The Astral Tide

The Astral Tide

by Alexandra Beaumont

The Astral Tide

Copyright 2025 © Alexandra Beaumont

This book is a work of fiction. All of the characters, organizations, and events portrayed in this story are either products of the author's imagination or are used fictitiously. Any resemblance to actual events or locales or persons, living or dead, is entirely coincidental.

All rights reserved. No part of this publication may be reproduced in any form or by any means without the express written permission of the publisher, except in the case of brief excerpts in critical reviews or articles.

Edited by Candace Nola

Formatted by Stephanie Ellis

Cover illustration and design by Alison Flannery

First Edition: April 2026

ISBN (paperback): 978-1-963355-54-3

ISBN (Kindle ebook): 978-1-963355-53-6

Library of Congress Control Number: 2026938424

BRIGIDS GATE PRESS

Overland Park, Kansas

www.brigidsgatepress.com

Printed in the United States of America

For those who fight on and stay kind when life is hard.

A Note from the Author on Her First Foray into Novels

The Testament of the Stars was written during lockdown: a strange fever dream of a time but felt like a great time to practice the art of writing a full-length book for the first time. I learnt a lot and since have moved on to my Myst Cycle series, which has been getting a lot of love for which I am very grateful. I am putting most of my effort into that world now, and that's a normal progression as an author.

Many people's first books aren't even published, so I am very grateful for Gurt Dog Press and subsequently Brigids Gate Press for taking *Testament of the Stars* on.

One of the things I learnt a lot about in writing this series is the type of character that people love to read. A lot of people said they loved Briarth most, and so I felt I couldn't not finish his story. Bri is an optimistic, cheeky, selfless character and I've come to really like him, so I wanted to do his story justice. It felt like writing Bri fanfic!

Another thing I've learnt is that it is very easy to burn out while writing and working full time, and that I have a tendency to commit to too much because I love writing. The outcome of this is that *The Astral Tide* is more of a series of vignettes or shorts about what happens to Bri and the people around him, so shouldn't really be read as a novel.

The path to success is paved by people supporting each other. I would never have managed this without the help of countless authors and friends who offered advice or read early drafts, my partner who edited my books around his editing contracts, *Alternative Stories and Fake Realities* podcast for making audio clips from the book, and the readers who took a punt on an indie author. Those people's kindness have shaped the kind of person I want to be, and I will always cherish that.

I hope you enjoy the end of this story, and let me say from the bottom of my heart—thank you for taking a chance on (and hopefully enjoying) the books that helped me learn how to write a novel.

This is an ending of a chapter of sorts, as I plan what I do next. Thank you for being part of this journey.

Prologue
~ The Drowned Star ~

I have watched you from the tides, and now is the time I will burn away the chaos and reclaim my people's blood. I will forge your thoughts in memories of those you love, words of those you will listen to and passions against those you hate.

In the shades of darkness where the star's tendrils shudder and tremble, reaching only with the strain of a thousand years' fragmentation of light, a man in tattered robes carves a four-legged beast with a two-tone tail into his acorn-hued leg. Looking up as the denizens of constellations dazedly gaze down, the man smiles. He does not know what awaits. The Time of Three approaches.

In the shadows of the coast, some way off, waves lap over the corroded crags of a fallen star-rock—vaster than any on land. A figure watches it from the shoals, ragged clothes encasing their body at strange angles as if they had not the knowledge of how to wear them. This body, unfortunate for the sailor who once owned it, but now possessed for a higher purpose. My purpose. The figure turns with a sigh and trudges up the rocky shore toward a glimmering forest on the horizon. It was time to leave behind the watery grave and right the cascading wrongs of this ill-begotten land.

I

Dying Dust and Dreams

~ BRI~

*Attend a tale written in the dust of your own ruin. The last tale of Briurth Arden,
failed politician and pointless optimist.*

The words came unbidden, dripping into my mind as if the droplets
of water seeping through the cracked ceiling of my small cell delivered
them. I leant back, parting my lips and gulping a tepid trickle of drips
down my raw throat. My once fine tunic and golden doublet had shredded
into ribbons and parted where the chains rubbed against my arms, clad
only in the musty silk that clung to my sweat-soaked skin. I had been alone
for days, weeks maybe. *Would Einya guess my gambit had failed? Would she try
to find me? I hope not.*

I'd made she sure was safe before I'd returned to our fallen home of
Gemynd and Rask, the once illustrious home to the stars, and that was
maybe the only thing I'd remembered apart from the whispered words I'd
said daily to hold onto what was left: *drink the stars, kill the queen, find the
cousin.* It was all I had left.

"One day I will write this tale for you, sister, just not until I know you
will not return here. This place is nought but decay," I muttered into the
gloom.

"Who are you talking to?" a voice said.

My head cracked against the wall as I twisted it quickly to find the
source. *Was it the queen?* One sharp tooth dug into my lip as I tugged
against the chains, trying to find her, trying to see despite the cloth
scratching my eyelids. When I'd returned and knelt to fool her, to try and
spy on the progress of the war, I'd never imagined I'd feel like this …

"Where are you? I can't see you …"

"You are blindfolded, you fool, and yet you could not find me even if you had use of your eyes," the voice said, a musical laugh within the words.

"You're not the queen …" I whispered, sagging against the chains, my head dropping down. "You're just a voice that keeps tormenting me, are you even real?"

"I am as real as you need me to be. Why are you still here, Bri? You will have no tale to tell if you never make your move. Give them something to fight for."

I lifted my head again, throbbing and wet at the back, trying to push away from the wall, but my body creaked and wouldn't move.

"The tale I wanted to tell is dying. I need the stars. Need to drink the Astamitra to stand any chance of doing what I must …"

"You'd take the star-blood drug again? To what end? You could be free of all this instead," the voice sang, taunting in a musical lilt.

"I can't be free until I kill the queen, kill the stars, and free the people from my cousin's rule. Kill her, too, if I have to," I rasped. "I need as much of the drug as I can … so don't cajole me from the shadows, whoever you are."

A soft sigh—*or was it a draft?*—brushed my cheek.

"Be careful. The queen grows tired of you, and you're running out of time. You need to make your move. Here she comes. Remember, everything is about the tale you will one day tell … be awake and aware enough to tell it. You're slipping, and you know it. Come find me when you're done."

"How can I find you, if I don't know who you are?"

"It pains me you don't remember, but one day it'll all come flooding back. Now *do* something."

The voice faded, slipping into the darkness for the mere drop of time left before the wooden door to the cell groaned open and a clatter of boots on stone echoed around me. Rough hands tore at the knotted blindfold, prising the coarse fabric from my eyes. From where I lay, sprawled on the grimy floor, I saw the Parlentan queen's embroidered boots first—grey and laced through with silver thread to depict the mountain home they'd left to invade mine. A flutter lightened the tightness in my chest. Craning my neck up to gaze on her, I swallowed. Her long hair was coiled up in a way that accentuated the soft curve of her slender neck. I craved to run my tongue along it—taste any Astamitra that might linger there. The floral scent of crushed star-rock, mixed with their copper blood, permeated the cell. The astrologers called it sacred, and craved it. To me it was nothing more than a drug I couldn't let go, thrumming through my veins.

Clawing my way upright, I clutched the queen's legs, my chains rattling as I hauled myself closer to her. The guards around her moved toward me, but she ushered them back with her slender, grey-hued fingers. Kneeling down, she pincered her hand around my face. I should have squirmed, should have wanted to pull away, but her grey eyes shone when I groaned. Her lips, slightly parted, close yet just out of reach.

"Star pet, are you ready to become one of us?"

"Ready, Glittering Majesty?" I stammered, breathless, knowing I had to say it though my fingers turned talon-like just at her presence. "I am ready, always ready."

"You know what to do then, little lordling," her honeyed voice whispered. "Check him, Mineral Master. Today is the day. I want to know he can take it. He is no good to us dead or half-mad."

"Half-mad serves us just fine. It has before. He is well enough, though his leg is bleeding."

Was it? I looked down, a fog clogging up my thoughts as I slowly remembered cutting the image there. Blood seeped through my breeches and trickled down my leg.

"How?" the queen demanded.

"Must have used a stone or something when we unchained him to eat. I'll check it."

Jolting, my attempt to jerk away when the Mineral Master came close did nothing. The queen held me tight.

"He's carved himself with a rough outline of some sort of animal."

"Don't touch that ..." I croaked. "It's my plan, my memory ..."

The manacles chinked against my trembling arms.

"Hush, hush, little lord. You have to stop hurting yourself. I need you. Do you understand?"

I preferred the mystery voice taunting me to her honeyed words, reminding me how snared I was. *Come back, voice.* Even so, my heart quivered in my chest as the truth tumbled out unbidden.

"I need you too. I'm sorry," I mumbled, resting my head on her shoulder.

"Little lord, what do you want, then?"

I swallowed. *Say it, I have to say it.*

"I have missed you ... please, give me the star-blood."

Her claws, I remembered those well. She ran her overlong nails down the side of my cheek as she always did. My lips parted, unbidden, and I leant forward despite the cutting metal slicing into my wrists. Her scent of damp rock and lilacs, achingly familiar now. I wanted it.

"Ask me for it, Briarth. Tell me what you want."

"I want you to pour the stars into me. I want you in my mind, seeing *all* of me. Take away who I was before, that man failed and I don't want to be him."

Even as I said it, I sagged forward, hair falling over my face while a tear tried to push itself from my eye. Dehydrated, it crystallised roughly on my eyelash and instead a sob dragged itself up my ragged throat. *Remember why you're doing this: use the stars, find your cousin, kill the queen. Stop her ruling Gemynd and Rask.*

"Please, give it to me," I groaned, wishing I was faking it like I'd originally planned.

"Then that is what we will do. Mineral Master, give me the vial."

A shuffle sounded, too close, and I wanted to pull away from the clinking glass. Another gulp, another tapestry of memories lost. *Don't do it …*

"Hush hush, Briarth, you want this, remember? I'm going to let you out of here. You can come be close to me. Would you like that?"

Her soft voice almost calmed me, and I forgot to writhe away. She tipped the tincture of crushed stars into my mouth. Then it all changed. Her claws dug into the bridge of my nose as she pinched it shut. Torrents of moisture welled up in my eyes while the crystal grit ground down my tensed throat, scratching the flesh inside as they scraped down into my stomach. I swallowed. Little pinpricks of pleasure seared my arms, and cold air sucked around my grinning teeth.

"Tell me how it feels?" the queen's voice said. It was everywhere now. Multiple pitches, pulsing around my mind.

"Like freedom …" I breathed, my mouth stretched too wide in its smile.

Someone was dragging me along, my feet scraping on stone until I crumpled to the ground and the scent of lilac returned as the queen brushed close. My arms ached as they bashed to the floor. Her lips touched mine, the grit of the stars dusted across her lips too. My hands reached for her, and she let them glide over her shoulders. Her own fingers ran down my chest, scratching flesh through my shredded doublet until I quivered. Hazy clouds drifted down around me as the stench of lilacs and copper forced their way into my nose.

"When did you release my wrists?" I babbled, realising I had reached for her freely.

"Hours ago, Briarth. Hours ago. You are free from your cell."

"I can't see," I said, reaching out. "When did I stop being able to see?"

"Your eyes are shut; you passed out. Open them fully, pet, you are one of us."

One finger lifted each eyelid, her skin clammy against mine, but I didn't flinch. Her angular face glared down into my eyes, yet her own grey ones were paler than I remembered. A circle of people in a large hall bedecked with grey and gold star-emblazoned banners of Parlenta watched. They'd brought me here, drugged, broken and unaware. The realisation brought bile to my throat. *What had I said when unaware? What had I done?*

"We, we are not alone?"

"No … why would we be? You are to be shown to your new people."

Her smile, wolf-like, kindled a fire that forced my heart to leap even now. The hall, more visible with each passing moment, bustling with Parlentans—soldiers and politicians alike. All with the grey eyes of star-drinkers. It was the Word Temple of Rask, but no longer. The pebbles that once told Raskian fortunes lay scattered around me, where I knelt.

"Look at me," the queen whispered. Tilting my head, her hand lifting my chin gently. My lips parted, watching her closely as she spoke. "He has grey eyes."

The proclamation, more for the room than for me, was loud. Piercing, even. A clattering applause sounded, flinching I reached to cover my ears, but she caught my hands.

"Let me in, like you said you wanted. Let me see *all* of you, for the first time."

Keep lying.

"I want nothing more."

They all watched, those grey-clad courtiers, glaring at me: a man in shredded colours, bent and hunched over, old before his time. I crumpled to my knees before her as she reached one hand toward me and raised my lowered head. Her lips graced mine, her breath—crystalline, like the stars—eased into me.

"Let go," she whispered. "After all this time fighting me, let go. Be at peace. Be one of us."

Sagging against her, thickness gripped my throat. My bleeding wrists and quaking body felt nothing to me. It was just me and her drifting between the stars as she held me tightly.

"Somewhere I'm tipping over a waterfall, tumbling back to you … you freed me from the mistake I made."

"You are one of us now, Briarth. One with me."

"I was always meant to be …" I mumbled, glancing up at her. "But what is the flash of orange, something in the distance, scampering away?"

Her fingers gripped my jaw, tilting my head up so my spine strained with the pressure. "Tell me what you saw."

My heart clenched, the thought slipped away, it, too, tumbling over the waterfall.

"It must just be me, the old me, leaving to never return. The true me joining you."

The queen smiled down at me, where I lay with my head resting in her lap and gazing up at her.

"Then it is time."

"Time, my queen?"

"Time for you to do my will. You will help us take the Gemyndian stars."

"I thought I had made a mistake. I can't remember what it was …"

"Hush, hush, would you displease me so soon after becoming one of us?"

"Not ever …" I swallowed. Something nagged at me. A voice? *Who was it?*

"Then come, my sweet Briarth. Let us get you dressed."

She offered me one hand, and I stumbled to my feet, leaning on her, but then courtiers flocked behind me and took my arms as the queen soared away amid congratulating courtiers saying words like 'converted' as I staggered in the direction the guards carried me. I crumpled slightly against the soldier holding me up.

"Don't leave me."

She turned, looking back over at me with a smirk that filled my heart with fire and fear.

"I will always be with you, little pet. Our stories align. You want to kill your cousin, and I need what she protects. Get it for me."

"How … how do you know?"

"You've told me every day: drink the stars, kill your cousin… remember?"

"There was something else too …" I mumbled. *Someone else I had to deal with?*

"Not that you ever told me," she said, smiling. "Trust me."

Then she turned, her gown whirling around her with a flourish, and my grey world consumed me. In the dust at my feet, I saw only one of the old word-stones from the temple: *Transformed.*

★ ★ ★

In my dreams the orange is there, but when I wake everything is grey. In the days that followed, I was given plain grey robes and taken to the edge of what once was Rask, the same soldier who had supported me when the queen left, gripping my arm and guiding me to a cluster of homes.

"This is where I leave you."

"This cluster of shacks?"

"Yes. Write a letter to your cousin. Tell her you want to meet."

"My cousin?"

"Yes. The printer will help you. Go inside. I have a question for you first, though," the guard said, leaning forward with pursed lips and eager eyes as if I was some kind of specimen. "How much do you remember? Are you truly her puppet, like the Mineral Master says?"

Running one hand over my eyes, I pressed them shut as a needle-like pain lanced through my brain.

"Nothing, except a mountain, some sort of animal and the queen. When will I see her again?"

"When you have delivered the star to her."

"But … that could be so long. How am I to do that?"

"That is not my problem. Go into the hut," he said, watching me as I pushed the door open weakly. Something familiar, a wrought iron mule nailed to the door, snagged my thoughts when I ran my fingers over it.

Inside a machine clacked away. Wood and metal pressed letters onto parchment in the bustle of a tavern. I took a slow breath, plucking at the tight sleeves of my grey robe. *This place …*

"Ah, one more to join our august company," said a haggard, grey-clad woman at the printing press who didn't even look up. "Best make yourself useful."

"Have I been here before?"

"Not that I'm aware of." She huffed. "One more to train."

A guard, sat drinking in a corner from a hipflask, glanced over.

"Raskian, this is the queen's pet. He is to write to Gemynd. To his cousin. To invite her to meet."

The Raskian woman at the press looked up then, hot eyes glaring at me. They weren't right, their colours different and strange. Blue eyes, not grey. Not normal.

"It's you …" she said, dropping the papers she worked so suddenly they scattered across the workspace as she lurched toward me. "What are you doing here? After all this?"

"Do I know you?" I stammered, raising one hand to keep the woman at a distance from me as my heart thumped at the back of my throat.

"Bri, it's me … we used to print together and …"

The guard laughed in the corner.

"He's a scramble now, print-woman. Belongs to us. He doesn't know who you are. He doesn't care."

"We used to print pamphlets," she tried again, bustling over and clutching my robe. "With Luskena. Remember?"

I just shook my head, but that name. *Luskena.* An earthquake of emotion spasmed through me, something clutching claw-like around my heart.

"I don't know that name."

Her hand dropped away from me, her shoulders sagging also as she sloped back to gather up her scattered papers.

"Then you are truly gone, like they say."

"Told you," the guard said, standing. "Now Briarth, write something to your cousin asking to meet. Hopefully, you remember her at least."

"I remember I have one … her name is missing …"

"Pearth Arden."

I nodded. My own name swam in my head: *Briarth Arden.* The guards said it to me at every opportunity. Maybe that was the only reason I remembered it. Crossing the room, I began to pick out the ink-covered blocks to type a letter. They stained my greying skin, dark blue against it as the metal blocks chinked against each other. My hands shook uncontrollably with each selection.

"What have they done to you, Bri?" the print-woman said, stepping closer to me again and putting one hand on my arm.

Looking down, I searched hard until I found an ironclad truth. My hands even steadied when my thoughts stumbled upon it.

"They made me whole. I carry no grief. The mistake I made: I don't remember it. I am here to make amends, and my queen has given me that."

"That cannot be true," she gasped, clutching my arm tighter. "I won't be part of this."

"I made too many mistakes. Let me send a letter, please, printer."

"My name is Paska. You knew that once, before it came to this. Our people carve steps for their army, Bri, and you pave the way with any letter you send for them. You open the steps all the way up to Gemynd. You would have cared about that once."

"I'm not the person you remember."

Paska's face wilted, a tear clustering in the corner of her eye, but she helped me select blocks when my fingers trembled too much to take the right ones out. Eventually, the letter was written with a few pointers from the guard who hovered at my shoulder, telling me to appeal to the love of my cousin. Paska bit out a bitter-laced laugh next to me at those words and looked away when I asked why. I read back the letter, wondering whether the words were mine—or those of the queen.

Dear Pearth, keeper of the Gemyndian stars,

My queen is here, and surrounds the settlement, but will cease her siege if you drain the stars and bring the Astamitra to her. We know there is something happening in Gemynd, but eventually you will need food. With broken promontories you must feel safe, but we are mountain people. The Parlentans, who I am one of now, are masters of mineral and stone. They are cutting a broad stair into the walls and soon their army will march into Gemynd. Come to the East of your settlement, you will see it for yourself, and we can talk.

If you are yet alive, meet with me to discuss terms, for all that passed between us and the love we shared as cousins. If Pearth is not yet alive, and another reads this, I have the same message: Bring the star—blood and save our people. Save Gemynd.

All my Love,

Briarth Arden

That evening, I watched the print-woman, Paska, and the guard attach several copies of the letter to a cluster of messenger pigeons which they cast up into the air. Originally, I'd tried to tie the letters myself. My fingers trembled and tore the pages as I tried to get them around the ankle of the flustered bird who beat its wings as if to get away from me—as if I were a fox come for my dinner.

"You may go now," the guard said after the letters were sent. "Return to the Word Temple, the queen might even see you."

"How can you be sure he will?" Paska spat, teeth bared.

"Look at his eyes. Can you really doubt it?"

Paska sighed and reached her fingers down to mine. I almost flinched back at any touch not the queen's. *What would she say if she knew another had held my hand?*

"He's right, isn't he? Word's curse, Bri. What have they done to you? Don't answer that, I don't want to know. Tell me this instead; where will you stay, where will you eat?"

"I … I don't know." I swallowed. Food hadn't even crossed my mind. The only hunger I felt was the absence of the glittering queen, gnawing at my stomach every moment of the day.

"I do," Paska said. "Come with me. No place is without the guards now, but at least we can get you warm and fed. You're skeletal!"

Looking down, I lifted the robe up slightly. My ribs protruded, dark like shadows against my skin.

"When did they get like this?"

"I don't know, Bri. I'll try to help if you'll let me."

She led me away and my brain felt like it twitched at every turn deeper into the settlement. The only salve was that there were Parlentan guards on every corner. I stopped briefly a few times, pulling away from Paska.

"Tell the queen I am eating, then I will be with her. Tell her I'll be with her."

Paska sighed every time and pulled me away.

"They don't care, Bri. Come on."

"She does. She does care."

"Yes, Bri, I am sure she does," she said eventually, squeezing my hand harder. "Why did you come back? I heard you'd left."

"I don't remember now …"

Paska didn't ask anymore. Instead we walked silently through twisting avenues that felt half-familiar for some reason. Eventually we reached a small building that was loud inside, like some sort of a tavern with a hanging sign saying The Dead Mule on it in fading paint. A dull ache permeated its way down my chest as I stopped abruptly.

"I can't go in there."

"Yes, you can. She would want you to."

"The queen?"

"Obviously not. I don't mean the queen. Come on, you need to eat."

"I can't …" I took a step away. All thought of food had fled my mind, but I didn't know why. A tear fell down my cheek.

"I know it's hard."

"Please … tell me why it's hard," I stammered, a knot forming in my stomach. "I don't know."

"Because of Luskena."

The tremble came back, this time in my knees, and it took Paska to hold me up to stop me clattering to the cobbles.

"You keep saying that name. Who was she?"

"Your lady of mischief. You loved her dearly."

"Her face is just a shadow …"

"One day. One day she will come back," Paska said, tilting my chin up with one hand and smiling with a soft sadness in her strange blue eyes. "Now come on, let's take care of you."

I stood, knees quivering like an earthquake as I stumbled into The Dead Mule. The noise inside was enough to distract me as I was guided onto a bench. The Raskians inside, all with their coloured eyes, stood and glared.

"Get out of here, grey eyes," one woman called. "You ain't welcome here."

"Who is this, Paska?" a man behind the bar said. "Why you bringing an outsider here?"

"He's one of ours."

"Looks like one of theirs," the barkeep said, circling toward me and lifting one of my eyelids to get a close look at my iris. I was so used to having them checked, I just slumped meekly and let him do it. Somewhere, a scream was sounding in the back of my mind, like something wild was clawing to get out. I swallowed and looked down at the stained table in front of me.

"Don't you recognise him? It's Bri. He's Luskena's Bri."

Suddenly a silence descended, eyes pinned on me like when I was in the Word Temple as the queen removed my blindfold. Then several voices began at once.

"That's Bri?"

"He's got grey eyes ..."

"He's dressed like them."

"We'll make them pay for this."

"The guards will hear us. Stop talking."

"We should cast him back to them."

I pressed my hands to my ears, rocking back and forth. Paska eventually whistled loudly, taking a step onto the bench where I sat and pulling my head to her leg to shut out some of the noise.

"Listen, friends, he is one of ours," Paska called out. "Luskena wouldn't have it any other way. After all he did for us, the least we can do is give him some shelter and food. Is that not worth a bit of danger? After all he risked for us? He is still in there somewhere."

"He's been made to be one of them," the barkeep said. "That much is clear. Just see his eyes, his greying skin ... we will make them pay."

"Let him prove it. Let him prove he's in there somewhere," another Raskian said. "How can we tell he's not a spy for them?"

Paska untangled me from where I clung to her. I'd not realised, but tears blotched my vision as my chest heaved unevenly. She softly placed her hands on my cheeks, tilting my head up to hers.

"Can you do that, Bri? Please. Tell them something that shows you're still in there. We used to be friends, remember? You flinch whenever I say Luskena's name. Show them you remember."

Paska supported me as I stood up, numbly gazing at the sea of judging faces. Something painful rose like a tidal wave bursting coastal defences, a sharp gasp burning my throat as pain shuddered through me. A flash of orange pulsed through my mind, bringing the memory back like a cascading rainfall.

"I can't remember her name, but ... I gave her a silver tree pendant. She ... she used to call me troublemaker. That's all I remember. I'm sorry."

Silence held. The barman strode over to me, face sagging and lips down turned. He held a small leather box in one hand. I froze, statue-still, as he brushed my matted hair from my eyes with his spare hand.

"It is him," the man said. "I can see the troublemaker in there, faded, but there. She wanted me to give you this, Bri ..."

The Raskian's eyes burnt into me, but I had eyes only for the little box the barman held out to me. Paska next to me squeezed my elbow as I took the box. My name echoed in my head again, remembering all the Parlentan guards saying it, as I saw the emblazoned B.A. on the box. My trembling hands prised it open. Nestled within was a ring with a silver leaf carved into it. Finely scrawled words, engraved inside, read:

My Troublemaker.

II
Echoes

~ BRI ~

The guards came into the bar soon after but stood at the edges of the room. I was a stranger again to them. It was clear in how they acted. In the busy tavern, I sat alone with a bowl of broth that tasted the finest I'd ever had. My stomach groaned and clenched with each spoonful, so I sat slumped against the wall, taking a bite and then waiting a long gap before trying again. I thought I'd seen Paska and a few of the others glancing with a soft pity in their eyes, and every so often I closed my eyes to stop me seeing it. In my spare hand, I clutched the ring box tightly. This had meant something, once.

After I had finally eaten, I staggered over to the guards.

"Does the queen have need for me tonight?"

"Now you want to return? You didn't come back last night, like you were meant to. We'll take you back when you leave here."

"Then why aren't you taking me?"

"We need to eat, too, star pet." One of them grabbed my arm, jerking it round and forcing me to reveal the ring box. I bared my teeth, curling my fingers over it. "What's this? A gift for the queen?"

"Please, I …"

"It's mine," Paska said, stepping up as if from nowhere. "I dropped it. He must have taken it."

The first guard sneered, but the second leant in close.

"Give it back, star pet. We can't be losing the goodwill of the printer. We need her."

I nodded, numb, forcing the relief back down. I couldn't risk the queen discovering there'd been another; that this Luskena had meant something to me.

"Thank you," I whispered, after I shuffled over to Paska and pressed the ring into her hand. She just nodded.

It wasn't long until the guards finished their drinks and food.

"Get out into the street then, pet," one growled, buoyed along by the alcohol coursing through his blood. A sharp elbow shoved into my back as I stepped over the threshold, forcing me into an uncontrolled stumble forward into the cobbles. My hands came away grazed and bloodied, sore like my head always seemed to be these days. The Raskians watched through the door, amongst them I focused in on Paska with her knuckles paling white as she gripped the door frame.

"Let … this be a lesson," the second guard drunkenly babbled. "Help us or become like him: forced to do the queen's will."

Forced? I swallowed.

The two drunk guards dragged me up, jostling me along the streets back toward the temple. Light rain made the cobbles slick, and I skittered here and there, uncoordinated. Every time I fell, I rolled over to get my face off the wet cobbles. The final time in the shadows of an alley, a cloaked figure watched. All I could see were two eyes in the pale moonlight spilling over the fields. Pushing myself up on blood-soaked knuckles, I glanced out to the fields, I could run … but the guards heaved me up.

"Come on, get yourself moving."

I thought about the idea as they dragged me onwards: running to barren fields with nowhere to go or returning to the warming side of the glittering queen. There was only one choice. A deep breath spurred me on the last little way toward the temple, thinking of her lilac-tasting lips and how I could feel again the sensation of her pouring star-blood into me like a waterfall filling a pool.

✭ ✭ ✭

She was there when we shuffled inside, raised upon a grand seat placed at one end of the hall. I shivered as she glanced at me, and all memory of the ring faded as I pulled free of the guards and lurched toward her. She ushered people away from her to let me get close.

"Did you do it?"

"I sent the letters," I rasped.

The queen tipped her head to one side. I instinctively lifted my chin to expose my neck for her caress as she raised one hand toward me, her long nails digging into my cheek as she pulled me close. She smiled, full rows of teeth on show.

"Very good, Briarth. Now, tomorrow, you will come with me to make demands to your cousin. For now, you will stay close by my side. I cannot have my prize slipping away, can I?"

My lips twitched as if part of me held back, but I grinned.

"I would not leave your side."

She nodded, and the sounds of shuffling echoed around me as all her courtiers save for a few guards left the hall.

"Bring my chaise in," she called, tugging me close and stroked my hair. The guards bustled about, readying what I could only assume was her bed behind an elaborate screen painted with stars above a mountain. "Tonight, my pet, I want you to dream of all you will do tomorrow. Not of me, but of what you will do for me."

"Let me be close, please," I choked slightly, something clawing its way up my throat.

"You will be. Come this way."

Standing, the grey-skinned queen stretched her lithe body, so her dress slipped slightly down her shoulder. My fingers tingled. I clenched my fist, resisting reaching out unbidden. She wrapped her hand into my robe and tugged me toward her chaise even while the guards watched with smirks on their faces. The closest stood close by with a vial held in her hands. The queen sat on the chaise and pulled me down next to her, forcing me to collapse clumsily into the seat.

"Are you ready to dream for me? We will dream with the stars together, and I will show you what to say."

"Will you be there?"

"I'll show you the path, give you the words. You will dream and know what to do."

I nodded, the guard nearby passing her vial to the queen. My eyes fluttered shut, lips parted, ready for the clashing silken voices and screaming instructions that would pour like a sweet abyss through my mind. The warm glass pressed to my lips, followed by her lips as she sealed the deal and pinched my nose again, so the crystal gritty liquid churned its way down my throat.

"Sleep," she bade.

"My troublemaker …" I babbled, as I sunk deep into the pool at the bottom of the crashing waterfall.

Gossamer hands with long claws

> *beset my face*
>> *as I*
>> *hang*
>> *from*
>> *the*
>> *walls of somewhere I've forgotten …*

The voice is back, echoing in the cell, but I am not in the cell. "Choose your own path." But I am with **her,** *and she is everywhere. The stars' truth, so close … but beyond an echoing chasm I cannot cross.*

Somewhere,
> *Somewhere?*
Somewhere,
> *Where?*

> *It's something different now,*
> *something rustles,*
> *pressing to my cheek.*
> *It will not let go of my scent,*
> *The scent of the stars.*

✵ ✵ ✵

In the morning, I woke with a scream ripping apart my throat, sprawled on the cold stone floor beneath the chaise.

"I can't see …" I babbled, scratching at my eyes to pry them open.

"There is a cloth over your eyes, Bri."

I noticed it: damp, dripping water into my eyes.

"Paska?" I stammered, clutching one hand blindly at whatever I could reach.

"You know me?"

"Yours is the only voice I know, apart from *hers.*"

"Hers?"

"My queen."

"Of course … I just thought you might have meant …" Paska said, voice fading. Gently, she peeled the cloth away, revealing the hall to me. Spots of lights, star-like, spiked through my eyes.

"Why are you here?"

"They fetched me last night. I found you gibbering and vomiting in the dark … alone."

"My people didn't look after me …?"

"They're not your people, Bri. Your queen wasn't here. They told me to keep you alive, or I'd take your place."

"Can you bring the fever down?" A nearby guard said, hovering over us both at the chaise. "The queen needs him today."

"I cannot guarantee he will walk far."

"He will have to. He's going to the brink of the stairs to Gemynd, as far as they have been widened."

"You'll make him even more ill …" Paska snarled.

Their words scattered around me, much as the word-pebbles on the floor of the temple, but none of them would focus for me as I stared down to the ground.

"I will go."

"Bri, you need to rest …"

"No," I snapped, glaring up from where I lay. "I will not have my choices spoken for me. I will make this choice. I must do this."

"This isn't your choice … they've made it for you."

"It is mine."

The guard stepped closer, but Paska's body tensed over mine.

"He is *sick*."

"Concern yourself with making him well again, then. That's why you were brought here in the night. He has made his choice. Honour it, printer."

Shaking my head, a shudder quivering through me, I reached out to push Paska aside.

"I am not sick. I need the stars."

"Bri … you will not come back from this. They are destroying you," Paska said, clutching me as I tried to stand up. "I cannot let you. Luskena would not let you do this to yourself. You always hated the star-blood …"

The guard breathed over us, so close the breath brushed over my sweat-slick skin.

"If this Luskena loved me so, she would know I had a plan. And this is my plan. If I convince my cousin to give the stars over, I will have more Astamitra. I will be well."

"This is folly …"

"No, it is a truth I should have seen years ago. With it, there is truth. I am glad I went to Parlenta. There, I found righteousness."

In the shadows, a soft clap sounded, and the click of heels on the stone floor sounded. The queen, dressed differently now: crimson. I'd never seen her in colour before.

"Bravo, sweet Briarth. Come with me, I have something for you."

I followed her, sparing one glance to Paska, who knelt with a frown marring her face as her nails dug into her legs. I dragged my eyes away, stumbling after the queen.

In the annex to the hall, a fine silken doublet rested on a cabinet—crimson as well.

"Put it on," she said, lifting it and holding it out.

Wordlessly I did, and as a servant stepped forward to button the doublet up a thought dug through my mind like a maggot, worming its way into my thoughts. I shoved it away.

"I've done what you asked. I need some Astamitra. My hands tremble, give me some. Please."

"You will soon have as much as you need, when you tell your cousin to give us the stars."

"Please, some to get me there," I rasped, eyes wide.

"Patience," the queen whispered, pressing one hand to my lips. "Now, come. Are you ready?"

"Always, for you. I will get the stars for you, glittering queen," I said, swallowing. Raw or not, my throat felt cavernous without the grit of the stars churning down it. Even so, the name of the queen on my lips felt *broken* somehow.

Outside the temple, guards had formed up with a group of Raskians dressed much less finely than their Parlentan opposites. A palanquin, borne by four guards, waited and the queen strode toward it. Once we joined it, the procession began immediately. Paska walked with them, a few paces from me but glancing over. She carried in her hands the same bundle of wet cloths she'd had before, her fingers crinkled from long exposure to the damp. She was here to keep me going.

Next to me marched a guard with unkempt shaggy sandy hair, who wore strangely stained armour as if it hadn't been cleaned after it had last seen combat.

"How will we get up the stairs? Are they finished?" I asked, but no-one answered. The procession was silent save for a single piper up the front, presumably for the queen's pleasure.

Sweat beaded again on my brow, feet clattering over loose stones and large gaps in the road. Large flagstones had been pulled up, leaving a pocked and battered street. *For the steps,* I realised. They really had built a staircase for their army.

"One foot in front of the other, come on Bri," Paska said, suddenly at my side.

"I ... I can't remember what it's like up there. Didn't I used to live there?"

"You did, *hush hush*, come on. Just walk. Not much further to the wall, then we'll have a break as they smash down the barrier at the top."

"Barrier?"

"Yes, to protect themselves as they widened the final part of the passage."

"How long has this been happening?"

"Months ... all day and night, Bri."

"But I ... I've been here all this time."

"Then you really do need to cleanse your body of the stars ... you've become their thrall, Bri. I'm so sorry."

"I feel like I had a plan ... a reason why. Now all I know is I am going to kill my cousin and take the stars."

"Whatever it was, your plan has been lost to madness. To the queen's ego."

Paska tipped some water down my throat and made me eat a piece of dried apple that tasted like ash before hooking one arm under my shoulders and supporting me the last stretch of the walk.

Finally, by the looming walls, I sagged onto a rock. The guards set the queen's palanquin down, helping her out.

"Bring him," she said, gesturing back at me as she stepped toward the winding stair without a glance back at me.

"He needs to rest," Paska said.

"There is no time."

"You'll kill him," she growled, but I barely heard it.

The glittering queen shone in the emerging sun as she stepped over to me with the sweetest smile, just slightly revealing her dainty teeth.

"Briarth, a guard will help you up, alright? Then some Astamitra when you reach the top."

"Thank you," I whispered, smiling too. An ache twisted through my jaw, and I realised I'd been grinning all day.

The sandy-haired guard with the stained armour twisted one arm under me, and jostled me toward the stair behind the queen.

"I will be behind you all the way," the guard whispered in my ear and spoke a bit louder. "*Uh*, so best not try anything."

One step in front of the other at first, yet it didn't take long until I sagged forward to climb on my hands and knees, my vision swimming. What must have been a narrow spiral stair once was now roughly hewn to be three abreast, and then Parlentan guards and courtiers scaled it easily.

Distantly, a faint voice thrummed through my mind. Was it mine? *This isn't a diplomatic visit; this is an occupying force.* I couldn't think about that. My knees trembled and my insides twisted like a whirlpool.

"One more step, and then star-blood. One more step, and then star-blood," I muttered over and over. The sandy haired guard behind me often had to lean forward and heave me upright, arms around me to keep me steady as my arms quivered and buckled beneath me. His armour spiked against my back, digging deeply into my shoulder blades, but I couldn't say anything except my repeated mantra.

At the top, the way was barred. The collective of Raskians were smashing down their makeshift barricade with lump hammers.

Slumped on the stairs, the Parlentans stepped over me to reach the top until I was the last at the rear of the force with only Paska and the scruffy guard for company. Deep breaths, laced with the lilac and damp stench of the stars, pulsed up from my lungs—ragged and uneven. A russet flash skittered up the stairs and then retreated back a pace as I spotted it, an overlarge orange-and-white tail disappearing back down the stairwell.

"Wait," I croaked. "I saw you in my dream ..."

"No-one is there, Bri," Paska said, crouching down and brushing the hair from my eyes. "It's just us."

Above us, a crack shattered through my dulled hearing. It took a few moments before I realised that I'd gripped my ears with hooked hands and only released them when the gentle fingers of Paska prised them away.

"Why are you doing this for me?"

"We can't let you go there alone after all."

"Why?"

I looked up at her face, still smiling despite it all. The guard and the Raskian exchanged frowns.

"You would have done it for us, once," Paska said.

"Maybe. I don't know what I would have done."

I turned away, but with their help and my hands tracing the rough-hewn wall, I staggered the final paces into the grey smog and dust of the cracked open barricade. My hands held out before me, I searched for the crimson dress of the glittering queen somewhere in the powdered dirt of destruction.

III
Gambit

~ BRI~

As the dust cleared, the wide streets sprawled before us, beams and windows scattered across the cobblestones and furnishings flung from buildings to block doors. No-one was there.

"My queen," the Mineral Master I remembered all too well said, "they have not come."

"I can see that, Jaquard." The queen's teeth bared, unpleasant for the first time.

I flinched back. It was as if beneath the finery, a beast hid.

"Something is not right," I said, gazing out at a half-familiar street chequered with destruction. "Something happened ..."

"We shouldn't stay. This is a trap," the Mineral Master continued.

The queen took a few tentative steps forward, her crimson dress trailing in the dirt.

"What do you suggest, then?"

"Send me," the sandy-haired guard said next to me, too quickly. "I will find their leader."

"Wait, no, send me," I babbled, staggering shakily up to the queen and gripping her hand. "I will find the stars for you and return to bring the Mineral Master there once I know it is safe."

"You? You can barely stand."

"Then give me one last bit of star-blood, please, and I will get you more."

"Fine, one last vial for when you need it. You best return ..."

"I will make sure he does," the sandy-haired guard mumbled, reaching out to guide me back to sit down on nearby rock with a surprisingly gentle hand.

He suddenly froze, head snapping around in the direction the assembled crowd as a scratching sounded in a nearby building.

Trembles simmered through me, and I stumbled backwards. *Something was wrong.*

The furnishings across a nearby door burst apart, scattering splinters over cobblestones. Two flaccid-skinned figures with distended claws lurched through the doorway, snarling and stumbling toward the crowd of Parlentans and Raskians. Bodies began to writhe against each other to bustle toward the stairs, the guards huddling around the queen with each step. Reaching for my belt, as if a rapier usually sat there, I clutched at nothingness.

"Get back," the sandy-haired guard yelled, shoving me so hard I stumbled away and clattered clumsily to the cobbles. Rolling over, I heaved my way on hands and knees as the dull ring of steel unsheathed behind me. Glancing back, debris dust kicked up again in the chaos clouded my vision. The Mineral Master ran past me, following a cluster of guards who presumably gathered around the glittering queen. A wild, pulsing moment of instinct sliced into my heart, and my sharp-nailed fingers reached out, snagging the squat man's ankle. Surprise coursed through me as he stumbled to a stop and screamed. My teeth were dug deep into his flesh, thick sluggish blood glugging into my mouth.

"What are you doing?" he screeched, twisting, looking over one shoulder to where the beasts circled Parlentan guards.

Lurching back, I kept my hands wrapped around his leg but unclenched my jaw from his ankle—spitting blood onto the cobbles with a wrangled cough. *What had I become?*

"Give it to me," I snarled, looking up, my hands digging into his flesh. *How? They were too sharp, too long… to beast-like.* "Star-blood, give it to me."

The Mineral Master glanced frantically backward and dug one hand into a pocket.

"Here, wretch, now let me go."

He dropped the vial and it clattered to the street, little shards of glass burst around me. No moment to spare. The thick liquid began to seep from the broken bottle in between the cobbles, I ran my tongue through the gaps and in the shards. Dust, glass, and the sweet aromatic grit of the stars coating my tongue and scratching my throat as I swallowed it down. The Mineral Master hovered over me briefly, a sneer on his lips.

"That's more than we gave you in a month, so you best make good of it. Go find the stars, get their blood for our queen. Try not to die."

With that, he ran, leaving the guards to fight the beasts while he chased back toward the stairs the queen had fled down. None of it mattered, as silken-star voices fought for my attention as I lapped up the last of the star-blood. Every inch of me tingled, as if they stroked me and whispered in my ears.

"Move," a voice said. The voice from the cell again.

"Why are you back now, tormentor?"

"Because you lie here, dreaming of stars and cackling to yourself while your friends run from beasts."

"My friends …?"

"The guard and the print woman, Paska. Go, you fool."

Contorting myself and rolling over, I saw two beasts circling and the sandy-haired guard pacing back with a rapier raised and a chair in his left hand as a makeshift shield. Paska held the door of a wardrobe aloft, and a heavy claw from the beast fell on it and the woman who had helped me flinched backward.

"Get up, use all this star-blood. Do *something*," I muttered.

"Finally, you realise. Come on, be who you were," it said, then the voice was gone again, as swift as it had come.

Be who you were: brave. *You were brave once. Probably.*

Pushing myself up to my feet, elbows shaking, I took my weight and forced myself up, staggering forward. Each breath scorched my lungs, fire thrusting through them. Eyes wide, arms outstretched, searing light shattered through the twilight sky, bursting from me as a howl tore instinctively from my lungs. Voices, not the one from the cell, but *others* swirled through my mind—all of them saying the same.

Free us from the beasts.

I took a last lurch forward when the guard and Paska staggered away from me, shielding their eyes. One last burst of light pulsed from my mouth, blinding me as I sagged to the stones and a cacophony of crashing echoed around me. Silence settled in the street. My body curled in on itself, sobs rattling my ribcage at the pain, the light surged through me. I kept my lips sealed shut, nausea rippling through me. I had to control it, control myself. *Who even was I anymore?*

A soft hand touched my shoulder, gently squeezing.

"Look at me," a male voice said.

"You are not real," I stammered, daring to open my mouth as I quivered on the icy dust-coated stones. "Leave me alone."

"You half-blinded me, Bri, I assure you I am real. It was as if you burst those beasts …"

"We need to move. We can't know he'll be able to do it again if there are more," Paska's voice grated near my ear.

Four hands, gripping my shoulders, forced me over and held me down while I scrabbled against them. Around me, fragments of bone and strips of grey skin scattered and from the carcasses a smoke simmered upward to the sky where specks of moonlight burst through the smog cloud of the burning citadel.

"We'll have to drag him," the man said. It was the sandy-haired Parlentan guard.

"No, what are you doing? Did the queen send you?"

"I … I am not …" The male guard paused. "Yes, absolutely. She bid you let me guide you."

"Where? Why did she not tell me?"

"Would you have her in this danger?"

I shook my head numbly, even as they held my quivering shoulders down.

"His mouth is bleeding," Paska rasped.

"We can deal with that later."

A heavy cloud of stupor seeped through my senses. A fog thickened around me, cage-like, and I remembered only the fragments of their exchange as they heaved me up between them and dragged me through the streets with my feet trailing behind me. I clenched my hands shut, feeling sure a third person was there, drifting with us and holding my fingers tenderly.

You are not done yet, mischief-maker.

Falling: I was falling into a pit lined with bones. I flinched awake, twitching against something that held me in place. Sunlight leaked through a grated window, spilling through a thin pad of gauze-like material placed over my eyes.

"Help me," I stammered. "I can't move."

A weight rested beside me, softness at my back and a pillow beneath my head as awareness crept through me.

"Steady," a voice said. "I am going to remove the gauze. We need to talk. We have to get you back to being you again."

Burning sun seared my bloodshot eyes as the pad peeled away, and black spots whirled in and out of my vision. Two firm hands, either side of my face, froze my instinct to thrash back and forth. The Parlentan guard, with no armour on now but just a simple grey robe, leant over me. From his eyes streamed a grey dye, seeping the bland colour away from his irises to reveal a soft blue like the shoals of the coast a league from Rask that seemed a faint memory now.

"Do you remember me?" he said, still sat beside me on the bed and leaning over me. His right hand rested on my arm and a single finger twisted into the fabric of my robe.

"I … I wish I did."

Glancing around the room, looking anywhere to avoid seeing the pain in the strange man's eyes. A bowl full of sick struck through with speckled grit and glittering bile rested on a splintered side table. Above me, my numb wrists were tied with a strip of ripped cloth to the splintered bedframe and blood crusted under my long fingernails. As if connected, a stinging itch across my ribs seared suddenly and I looked down with horror lancing through me as strips of peach flesh had flaked away to reveal grey underneath it. Ragged breaths pounded through my lungs, burning tears spiking in my eyes.

"What is happening to me? Am I lost in the shades of darkness, where the stars struggle to tremble?"

"What do you mean? We don't know, but we will find a way, Bri. I promise." The guard leant forward, gently untied my wrists.

"What are you doing?"

"Hoping you're awake enough to not hurt yourself," he mumbled, leaning in and resting his forehead against mine, holding me so tight my feeble struggle faded against him.

Between staccato breaths, I managed to gasp the words that rested on the end of my lacerated tongue.

"Who … are you?"

"We were … I mean, we are close. As close as can be," he whispered, breath grazing my skin as we rested with our eyes shut. "My name is Prethi. I've been waiting here for you these past months, trying to get to you, hiding among the Parlentans. Paska told me where you were, we couldn't find you for ages and then suddenly you were there in the printing house. I could've laughed with joy."

"I wish I remembered you … you seem … warm."

"One day you will, when you are better."

A sob choked out of my lungs as I leant forward and tangled one hand in the man's robes, as if somehow that would help me remember. Prethi gripped me tighter, encasing me in his arms.

"I had a plan. I had a plan, but I can't remember it. I don't know if it's working. I feel like I had to wait. Wait for something to find me. What am I waiting for?"

Prethi leaned back where he sat on the bed, opening his eyes and wiping some of the dye seeping out of them from his cheeks.

"I don't know, but I'll tell you this: you're not Parlentan."

"No, Bri, I'm Gemyndian. We are … almost like family," he stroked one hand over my cheek, brushing away a tear. "I wish you'd never sent me away. I wish you'd told me your plan …"

"It's on my leg, that's all I know. I carved it into my flesh."

Prethi frowned, reaching a trembling hand toward me. His eyes stretched wide, and the man bit his lip as his fingers hovered above my skin.

"May I?"

I nodded, swallowing nausea again as he gently prised the blood-soaked fabric up my leg.

"A dog? Or a fox? Your plan is a dog or a fox?"

"Is that it? Is that all that's there? I'd hoped for …" I gasped, the swell of vomit pressing up my throat. *How could that be all?*

Prethi quickly seized the bowl and hooked my too-light body upright. He held me as grit, dust, and glass churned up my throat into the bowl.

"Ugh, I …"

"Get it all out, Bri. Be yourself again."

"My plan must …" I croaked between heaves. "Must have been better than this."

"It probably was, once."

"Why are you doing this? I'm a failure …"

Placing the bowl down again, Prethi pushed the hair from my eyes.

"Don't say that, don't ever say that …" he began to say, but I'd looked away.

Through the stained window, pricks of silver light shone. Their burning form curled like a beast: four legs and a long snout trembling in the night sky.

"It is time," I spluttered.

"Time? You have to rest, Bri. There's nothing else you can do while you're like this."

"I need to find the person they said is my cousin, I need to find the stars … so the stars can find me," I said, clutching Prethi's robes again as the room whirled around me and constellations gleamed delightfully on the walls.

"That makes no sense, Bri. Please, just lie back."

A door creaked open, sending a spasm through my spine as I flinched away until Prethi steadied my body again.

"It's just Paska, Bri. Don't jerk like that. Please. Your body is fragile."

"You … you came back for me."

"I …"

"Do something for me," I rasped, surging upward suddenly, wrapping fists in her shirt. "You see that? See those stars all on the walls? Find me those stars."

"Find you the stars?"

"I need them, I need them and the star-rocks. Please."

"What for?"

"Drink the star-blood, save Gemynd, find the constellation and be free … this is my plan. This is my plan."

Prethi's hands clenched around my shoulders, pressing me back down on the sheets.

"Bri …"

"No," I clamoured, struggling against his weight as he held me down. "You work against the queen, work against my plan."

"What's your plan, Bri?" Prethi whispered.

"His skin burns. He speaks of nothing," Paska's voice said somewhere near my ear, cold breath seeping over my face.

"Not nothing …" I said, my eyes fixed on the stars at the window. Remnants of my fading muscles writhed, legs thrashing. "I can see myself, from the stars."

"What, Bri? What are you saying?" Prethi said. "Paska, we're losing him, his eyes—they … the last colour is fading. They are almost white."

The brusque shaking of Paska's strong forearms gripping me and shaking me almost dragged me from the haze that had settled over me. It was not enough.

"I can't see your face anymore. I am above you. I am the Constellation …"

"What do we do when the queen returns?" Paska growled, her eyes suddenly wide. "She will not leave us alive, or him, if he is no longer useful to her."

"Trust me …" I said, letting my eyes drift shut.

The room churned around me as if I fell, but I tumbled upwards, not down, tipping over a waterfall again until I drifted, feather-light and lofty. Below me a fragile body thrashed amongst tattered sheets; it is both me and not me.

I am formless, I am the starlight.

Two frantic people bustled around the body that scrabbled and scrabbled at their faces with hooked claw-hands. The one dressed in

Parlentan robes desperately slaps the side of the man's face, calling a name I no longer remember. The man, with ribs protruding like a cage around him—locking in who he used to be—trembles and his eyes burst wide open. Guttural last words croak from his throat before he collapses into the bed.

"It is time. I know the path I take. I know your return will free me when all is said and done."

IV
Writing Stars

~ TOLLSKA ~

I crept into the star-rock glade, shadows sneaking from the darkness of the forest and concealing me as I wove between each canopy's cover to prevent the starlight touching me.

"What are you doing?" I hissed, baring my teeth.

The figure in the centre of the glade, swarmed by starlight where it spilled through the single gap in the thick trees, did not even twitch. Around her, the vines that burst forth from the fallen star-rock gathered and snaked over her wrists like extensions of her veins. I swallowed, acrid bile lurching up my throat.

"Einya, answer me, please."

My heart cantered in my ribcage. It had never steadied since the starlight had sliced through me back in Gemynd almost a year ago.

"Something is wrong," Einya gasped, tangled up in the vines creeping from the star-rock. I almost lurched toward her, but my feet stayed locked in the shadows of the trees. The circle of starlight cast down through the opening in the canopy created a stark threshold between the forest and the glade.

"What?" I said, warring desires to go to her and run the other way churning within me.

"A new constellation just burnt its way into the sky ... I felt it ... it watches ..."

Glancing into the starlit night from the darkness, a tremble spasmed through me. The pinpricks of oppressive silver light-like eyes glared at me. They know where I am, always.

"Don't tell me that, Einya."

"Tols … I'm sorry," she whispered, untangling ivy from around her wrists and stepping from the light until the shadows swallowed her.

"You promised me you'd stop talking to them."

"I know, but can't you see it? Look up, they are too bright, they are burning through the leaves above us …"

"You really don't know when to stop talking, do you …" I said, swallowing, my heart easing slightly as she stood here with me and her arms twined around me. Ice-like chill seeped over me at her touch, as if the starlight somehow moved with her into the shadows. "What does it mean?"

"Something is moving, something is coming. The stars reach toward their final gambit …"

"Oh, good."

"They are neutral, remember …"

"Sounds very neutral."

"You were amongst them, you know how it is …" Einya muttered, brushing one hand over my cheek.

"I am trying to forget. You promised me this would stop."

"I did, I'm sorry …"

"You're sorry, you're addicted, and now they reach back to you with their agenda."

"They take no sides."

She ran one hand through her russet hair, once coiled neatly at all times but now left loose to blow in the breeze. I sighed, tangling my fingers in hers. Her eyes didn't meet mine.

"I still want to kiss you, even when you're an idiot," I whispered, gazing at her star-drenched eyes with dilated pupils watching me like the stars did.

"I am always yours, first and foremost," Einya said, stepping closer.

"Then come into the shadows with me."

A soft nod rubbed against my cheek, and we plunged backward into the canopy's anonymity, veiling the eyes of the stars as our bare feet scattered leaves and pressed moss between our toes with each step.

"Where are we going, Tols?" her voice called behind me, cold somehow.

"Where we always go."

Eventually, in the thickest canopied part of Aisren, I finally stopped. Our familiar den of long sticks resting on a leaning tree trunk emerged out of the lingering darkness. Ducking into the entrance, I pulled her behind me—our hands firmly clasped together. In the petrichor-scent-laced hideaway we slumped on the fern-scattered carpet, lips inches from each other's as a soft pattering of rain trembled on the leaves above us.

"This is all need," I whispered.

"And me."

"Shining Einya."

"Mysterious Tollska," she croaked, her dusky lips gently pressing into mine.

"Come closer …"

I snaked my hands around her hips, tugging her close, shoving away the thought of the vines from the star-rock clambering over her with a pang striking at my heart.

"I need to tell you something," Einya said, one hand pressing against my shoulder and forcing distance between us. "To ask you something."

"What is it?" I whispered, trying to shuffle closer again. Even here, in the darkest thicket of trees, night felt bare and treacherous.

"Their voices never really left. Not entirely."

"But …"

"They are louder now. I felt the tug again. I had to listen."

This time I pressed myself back from her, glancing down to where her hands twisted in her long scarf as I shifted away.

"Tols, please …"

"I should have known. Once an astrologer, always an astrologer. Where does this end?"

"I don't know, that's what I need to ask you … Bri left, and I don't know what's happening in Rask."

"We vowed our lives would be here …"

"And to that, I hold true. I'm not leaving."

"I would never make you choose between me and Bri."

"I know."

"Come here, silly star-botherer," I breathed, shuffling over the fallen leaves to wrap my arms around her trembling shoulders. "What do we do now?"

"I don't know. I don't even know what it means. I thought they'd left me."

"Maybe you're imagining sparks where only shadows dwell …"

"I just felt … felt like something might have happened to Bri."

The deep sigh that followed her words surged rapidly from my lungs.

"Go after him, though you know he would not want you to."

"I know, but what if …?"

"Just trust him. That's all you can do. What will you do from here?"

Her eyes briefly flickered away from mine, glancing back toward the star-rock glade before returning to mine.

"I am here for you, always, Tollska. I am sorry."

"Be with me then. Please don't fall back to the stars. I thought you said Breyneda told you'd they'd fade."

"Maybe there's a reason they haven't."

"I can't lose you," I stammered, my muscles tensing as I held even tighter. "WE can't be snared by the stars again."

"I promise we won't lose each other," Einya whispered, running one hand down the side of my face. "I won't let them anywhere near you."

Eventually, my eyes drifted shut as we embraced in the cloak of the forest and fell to sleep in the only place the stars could not see us.

~ BRI ~

A tide of tingling pulsed around my body when something nudged against me, waking me from a stupor where I lay coated in the dirt of a side alley from the crumbling Gemyndian buildings.

"Where am I?" I tried to say, but a strangled yelp was all I could manage.

My body was too small, my hands tiny as I lifted myself onto all fours to scramble out of the small hole I must have clambered into. A ripple of tension stiffened every hair on the back of my neck. Something was watching me.

"Get out of the shadows," a voice growled, as if it was by my ear or in my head.

How had I got here?

Stumbling forth, the rubble scratched at me, but somehow it didn't dig into my flesh. A jitter sliced through my belly and realisation crashed over me: I was too low to the ground, and in my panic, claws flexed out of the pads beneath my feet, scraping the stones I stood upon. I opened my eyes and saw russet-furred paws against the dusty cobbles.

"Don't panic, little troublemaker," the voice said, unlike before the melodic ring echoed and clutched at my memory. "This was your plan. Get to the stars. It is time to hunt, time to make this right. You carry my Bri's memory, and he carries the stars for you. Together, you will be one."

Lips peeling back from my teeth, glancing around, no-one was there, but a sudden warmth crept through me and the plush tail behind me flicked back and forth. Grinning. I was grinning. No more a frail man in skin too tight. My body pulsed with strength, instinct, and energy. Passion burnt through me, a memory of fighting for righteousness with every last shard of my being. No more waiting.

I burst from the shadows, four legs padding with a speed that only widened my wide fox-toothed grin as I scampered through shadows and into the night. It is time.

The fevered speed only lasted faded, instinct creeping over me. The towering buildings and crumbling streets felt strange as I looked up, regarding them all from so low and along the long snout between my eyes. The balustrades and gargoyles, distorted by wide eyes and a gossamer sheen that coated every surface. Fate did not weave me enough time to contemplate the new sights and scents to my heart's content, but I wandered for half a day with sharp eyes—weaving in and out of nooks in buildings and contorting myself through cracks into cellars.

Eventually, I found my way into the wider streets, drawing me intently toward the tower that twisted in my memory with a scent of resentment for something that I couldn't quite recall. A time when I collected someone from here. The person was addled as I now was, maybe? All I remembered was supporting someone, their arm thrown over my shoulder as we staggered together and my heart ached for their loss of freedom.

A shudder ran through me, and although I was still bound in fox fur and padding through the streets on all fours, it was as if I could see my real body writhing in the bed at this sight. Tears streamed down the strange man's face, but I shook my head, thrashed it back and forth as if I'd gripped a rabbit in my teeth and I was shaking it dead.

"That's you, Bri. The body is you. You have to hold on," the voice whispered, stalking me everywhere I went. "Don't you forget that's you."

I ran out of time to hunt down the strange drifting words. As I twisted around, trying to find them, my hackles quivered and I hunkered into a crouch. From by the tower, a crackling scream battered my ears until I folded them back to shut out some of the sound. The crinkle of the flesh around them sent a pulsing shudder through me at the peculiar sensation of being able to control my ears like that. One of the beasts that seemed but a fragment of a memory lurched out from a building, dragging a young male behind it, long talons and slathering tongue glistening clearly even at this long distance.

"Free them," the voice said. "You wanted to free them all."

"I know," I tried to say. Only a yelp sounded again.

Paws flexing, distending, until claws slipped knife-like out of the pads, I lowered my head. Power coursing through my legs carried me rapidly, and the beast saw me only too late as I launched up and sunk teeth into the outstretched arm that loomed over the child. Star-grit fused in thick, treacle-slow blood slipped in heavy glugs into my mouth until the beast swung round and the momentum broke my grip, dropping me to the cobbles in a furry slump.

The child was free, cowering against the rubble. The beast circled me with glowing eyes and flexing its hands ready to strike. A tidal surge of strength throbbed back through me. I launched again at the beast. The lurch was sudden, as its own torrent of energy pulsed forward. I rolled to one side and back onto my paws. Tension trembled through my body, an audible crackle ripped through my mind until I squeezed my eyes shut while waves of starlight burst from me and I leapt forward blindly. My ribs rattled when I collided with something, making me think of the weak human body I'd left behind, but this was different. The thrumming of stars searing around me thrust me forward like a gust tugging me over a cliff, and suddenly there was silence.

Something had happened. My snout was drenched in the thick, glistening star-grit-laced blood as I lapped it up from wounds I must have made. Each glug tasted like chewing down the freshest meat. My gekkering continued in a high pitch chitter at each euphoric mouthful. This was it: *this is how I win, by taking every scrap of the stars into myself.* I'd known it before. How had I ever forgotten?

"Back," a female voice shouted, sprinting out of the shadows. "Get back, fox."

Her bloodshot eyes fixed on me, rapier raised in one hand, and I rounded on her and glared intensely back. Head lowered, I appraised each inch of her. She'd waited to see me destroy the beast before coming forth, but now she advanced with the precision of a practiced soldier. Her blade flicked forward in warning. I skittered backward with claws scrabbling on the stones.

"Are you alright?" the woman called to the cowering boy, who crawled toward and eventually staggered to his feet. "Get behind me."

"I didn't mean to put you in danger ..."

"I am of the guard. I am meant to be in danger ..."

Surprise shuddered through me.

"I'm here to help," I tried to say, but a panicked high-pitch gekker split the silence instead.

The distraction was the split second she needed, as she lunged forth. Throwing down her rapier, large and strong hands gripped me tightly before I could wriggle away.

No matter how hard I snapped and writhed, her strong arms would not budge, and the more I tried to pulse light from me, the more I realised the truth. I, Briarth Arden, was just a passenger in my fox friend. Here to show him, or whoever controlled him, the way ahead.

"Are we going to eat him?" the boy rasped, eyes wide.

"No. You see how the fox destroyed the beast?" the soldier said. "He is going to protect us from them. Grab my sword, let's go. Pearth would want us to use him, let him protect the rest of us."

I yelped at the name. Strength, or perhaps will, ebbed out of me and I sagged in the warrior's arms—just like my real body, collapsing in on itself with all the pressure I'd put it through.

Sometime later, after the pair dodged through back alleys around the edge of the tower until they reached a small crack in its base surrounded by rubble and scattered wooden carts, the pair stopped.

"Check there's no-one following us, drop your bag in and come back," the soldier whispered.

The boy looked around and nodded, before slipping a bag off his shoulders and squeezing through the small gap into the darkness beyond. When he'd gone, the soldier grabbed me gently by the scruff of the neck, careful to avoid my teeth as she placed me on the ground and held me against the blood-stained cobblestones with one strong arm. The beat of a struggle writhed within me again, each movement the soldier made was done with care. She gently lifted my paws, wincing as I scrabbled at her with desperately flailing claws.

"Sorry, fox," she said, "but this has to be done."

Two rows of my sharp fangs emerged from behind my thick lips, snarls burning the back of my throat when the soldier pulled a belt from around her waist. As soon as the boy slipped back through the crack, she nodded and between them, their hands tightened the belt around my neck and knotted the other end to a rotting cart that part-concealed the crack into the base of the crumbling tower.

"That should do it," the boy said, not so young now I saw him up front—just painfully thin. "Will it work? Will he keep them away?"

"It's worth a try."

Please … I tried to rasp. *You don't understand …*

Only snarls came out as they clumsily straightened out, as if even standing made them ache with fatigue. I flexed against the belt, trying to pull away, though I was firmly held in place.

Don't leave me … I saved you …

But they left, clambering through the crack and leaving me howling in the empty street as even then the glowing eyes of the beasts loomed close around me.

✯ ✯ ✯

At some point as dawn crested, sun soaked my russet fur, and I trembled. I'd not slept but had found a way to curl up even while the belt snagged me against the cart. In the small hours, as the last of the light faded, one of the grey-skinned beasts dragged itself toward me. Unbidden the starlight had burst from me and churned the beast away down the street, as if battered by a relentless wind. Hunger clawed at the inside of my stomach leaving me with two questions that shattered any calm I had left: how many times could I do this? And, when I couldn't anymore, what would happen when I died in the body of a fox?

The voice who'd taunted me in the cell and followed me everywhere left me whining in silence until eventually a shuffle sounded inside the crack into the tower and the soldier from last night squeezed out with someone behind her. Both were wearing stained doublets studded with sapphire stars. The closest crouched down. Tilting my long face up toward her, I tried to make out her face through the soft gossamer filter that permanently glazed my eyes over.

"So, this is the fox … strange."

"Some of the guards have said they've seen it for weeks, stealing food and seeming to search for something. This is the first time it has come close. First time we've seen it attack a beast."

"How did it do it?"

"With teeth, and a light that exploded from it. It was like it tried to save Marthis."

"Well, we can make use of it."

The closer guard leant in then, gazing deep into my eyes just far enough away that I couldn't snap out and bite her. *Wait.* Something spikey snagged in my throat, a little gekker seeped out from between my teeth.

Her cropped straight hair and frost-laced eyes … *You …* I meant to say, recognising her at last.

I strained against the belt again, feeling it dig into my matted fur. Ice-laced fury tore at my heart. My cousin caused all this, and here she was, and I could do nothing.

"What's got him going?" the other soldier muttered, gesturing at me where I flailed at them and thrashed my head.

"Maybe he knows we don't have much time here with whatever power he has," Pearth said. "We'll move on again. The beasts know we're here."

"The sick are not getting any better, we cannot risk …"

Pearth looked at the older soldier, running one hand over a grime-soaked face.

"Until we finish the tunnels, we have no choice. If we go by day, it will be better. There's something I want to try first."

They shared a nod and, before long, calls went back down the tunnel and a ragged group mixed in age staggered one at a time out of the tunnel. Many were barefoot and limping. Some had tried to fashion makeshift shoes out of reeds or some kind of plant, but those, too, had quickly frayed away to tatters.

"Bring the fox," Pearth said, leaning down close to me.

Another frosty shudder trembled through me. I remembered her standing at the altar, taking Tollska from Einya. The names washed over me with a crashing certainty. My cold-hearted cousin had almost destroyed my sister, setting in motion a terrible cascade of events. I swallowed, remembering events that I compounded when I ratted her out to Parlenta.

The nearest guard untangled the belt from the cart and gently tugged on it. A quiver of curiosity flicked my tail up behind me. *They're taking me to the star.* So, I held down my desire to snap and bite. This was all I needed. *Get the star, take it back to my withered human body.* A powerful scent, floral and musky, twitched my nose as I crept forward. As we passed struggling men, women and children limping up the cave, Pearth stopped at every one—helping some by and digging morsels of food out of her deep pockets and passing stale looking bread to the frailest among the company.

A yelp strangled its way out of my lips as we entered the centre of the underground hovel they'd hidden in. A pulsing glow trembled at the centre of the room, and I tried to drag myself toward it, eyes wide and saliva soaking the fur on my chin. *Star-blood.*

Pearth leant down again, watching me with sharp eyes.

"You know what it is, don't you?"

I just pulled again until she let the belt go so that I skittered forward, the loose end of leather trailing behind me. Surprised, I turned back to look with one paw raised in uncertainty. My cousin just watched, her arms folded as her wayward group of ragged souls hobbled past her.

This was it. I could have it all, take it all to the glittering queen … do all I'd promised. Have as much as I wanted.

Even as I stood there, looking up at the glowing rock, I remembered something new … another memory washing back over me: my sister's body. Einya, twitching at the base of this towering rock, grit-fused tears running down her cheeks after she'd become an astrologer. I'd never told her how I'd cleansed the bile from her lips, rubbing it away with the hem of my finest tunic as I dragged her from the pile of spasming, newly appointed astrologers. I had wanted to come back for them all, take them back to their families and tell them how the stars warped their minds—and yet I never even told Einya. Now, here I was, worse than all of them—lost and crawling in the dust of our ruin as my body crumbled in the absence of my mind.

V

Lost Laments

~ TOLLSKA ~

Einya gasped, a tight breath sucking down her throat as she surged upright next to me, cracking her head on the wooden canopy above us.

"Tols," she cried, "I saw him …"

"What?" I said, reaching out and drawing her close.

"I have to go, I saw Bri …" she said, fingers fumbling to button up her top and grab her coat.

"Saw Bri, how?"

"He was with the stars. I don't know what it means."

I pressed my eyes shut. *Not again.* My hands shook as I grabbed my own clothes, and fire pulsing in my chest as my heart battered against my ribcage.

"I can't believe I'm going to say this, but let's go find him."

Einya whipped her head round, biting her lip until blood trickled down her chin. "You … we can't. I can't take you there. We can't go there."

"It would be my choice," I said, voice sharper than I meant it to be. "No, I mean you should go to the star here. If he's with the stars, they will know."

Einya pulled me close, our foreheads brushing.

"Thank you, Tollska. My heart is brighter because of you."

"Then let's do this and then leave it all behind. Go find out where Bri is."

We walked silently through the trees, at least sun speckled through the canopy rather than stars, and my footsteps felt lighter for it. At the glade where the star-rock held a lingering glow, even in the sunlight, I stopped at the threshold. A cold spasm ran up my spine, but Einya stole it away with a tight squeeze of my hand and a brief kiss before she crossed toward the star.

Her hands twisted in circles amongst the vines that clung to the rock as she knelt amongst the ferns that lived in the shadow of the looming stone. While she rested her forehead against the star, the vines twined into her braids until they appeared as one.

"Speak to me," she said, voice louder, echoing as if amplified by many voices.

Light brightened in the glade, making the forest around me seem darker by comparison until I shivered in the cold, I dug my nails into my olive flesh forcing red grooves into my skin.

"Einya, behind you," I called frantically. A figure sprung out of the growing light, vivid and burning around the edges. She didn't hear me, her head still resting in amongst the star-rock's vines, and as the creature reached a burning hand toward her, my feet fused to the forest floor. "Einya!"

Trembling flames, star-light up close, licked up her back, and a tremor rose in my chest.

"Get away," I snarled, and my feet suddenly shifted.

Running into the glade, bile surged up my throat, but I swallowed it down as I threw myself between the flaming star and Einya. My hands beat against Einya's back, scorching my fingers in the flames as I patted them out before lurching back around to block the creature from harming her again. The figure stood there, a smirk on its face as she ran one hand through curled hair that glimmered from within.

"It wouldn't have hurt her, I just need her attention," the figure said, voice metallic somehow but familiar.

"Do I know …?"

"Yes. Or you did once."

Curled hair, facetious, dead … it could only be one person. The séance, or whatever this was, seemed to be working.

"Luskena …"

"The very same." She chuckled, though it sounded unnatural. She bowed mockingly. "Now get Einya to talk to me."

"You're … how are you doing this?"

"I'm only dead as far as the stars ever let me be, since your dear spouse made me part of them."

"Not my spouse … I didn't ever want to be with Pearth. Not really."

The starlit outline of Luskena shrugged.

"Einya. Now."

I dropped one hand down onto Einya's back where she still rested trance-like against the star and shook her gently, not taking my eyes off Luskena.

"Tols ..." Einya muttered, clutching my hand and rubbing it gently as she stepped in front of me.

I wrapped my arms around her and rested my head on her shoulder, a trembling gratitude bubbling through me at the shield she'd made herself.

"Einya Arden, the one who was supposed to deliver us. How is that going? The pair of you, the astrologer and the sacrifice ... what a team."

"Don't," Einya growled, hand tightening around mine.

"Peace, I'm here to help."

"How?" I said, unable to resist. "Seems you're here to taunt us."

"Do you know where Bri is?" Einya said, her breath hitching and her shoulders quivering, where our bodies pressed together.

"He's got himself into a right mess. Always did without me. I've been a voice in the shadows, trying to remind him not to just drift into the nothingness of another well-meaning, badly thought-out plan."

"You're guiding him? Does he know?"

"He is too much of a mess to know," Luskena said, the strange astral form flickering as if anger or sadness coursed through it.

"What's he done?"

"I'm not sure. I only know he needs to go find his body."

"What?" Einya said at the same time as me.

"Yes, he tried to get close to the stars. I think he had a plan, something to do with a fox."

"Quandary ..." Einya whispered. "He told me about the fox, but not what he's planning. I need to help him."

The outline of Luskena flared, flames rippling around the edge as Einya and I lurched away.

"What, and run three days to Rask?" Luskena spat, "What then? Will he still be alive?"

"I can't just leave him ..."

"There's only one thing you can do."

One hand reached out, still glistening with minute specks of flame. I lurched forward, the heat tingling across my body as I pressed in between Luskena and Einya.

"What are you doing?" I hissed.

"Guiding the way. The only thing you can do is destroy the star here. Something is coming ... a reckoning. I can feel it now. The stars eat away at me, telling me it is on its way. A creature is coming to you. He will find Bri and get him to end this."

"Destroy the star?" Einya said behind me, crisp words dripping with ice. "How can you ask that? Get out of here. What would it even achieve?"

"Maybe getting rid of them would loosen their grip on all of us."

"Einya ... maybe it's for the best," I whispered, placing one hand on her arm, but she ripped it away.

"No, Tols. Bri turned against the stars and now look at him—caught up in some crazed plan to do who knows what with the stars even though he didn't trust them. If we had just sensibly used them in moderation, none of this would have happened."

"You didn't trust the stars either. You said they were a means to an end ... how can you advocate for their use now?"

"You don't understand. I saw what they could be, what they can be."

Einya surged forward, and I didn't grab her fast enough before she launched at Luskena with hands glowing. Eyes flicking shut and hand raised, I tried to reach for her with my other hand but couldn't find her. When the shining dulled and ceased pulsing rays of light through my closed eyelids, I opened my eyes and tried to see what happened through the black dots swimming in my vision.

"Where is Luskena?"

"Gone," was all Einya said.

"Gone, how?" I said, voice trembling. *What had happened?* "We have to do something."

My fingers looped around her wrist, gripping tightly to prevent her pulling away.

"What would you have me do?" Einya snarled.

"This isn't like you. We'll think of something."

"There is no time. A reckoning is coming, remember? I might not like her, but she's right. Something is coming."

"How do you know?"

"I can feel it as well."

"Is that why you don't want to destroy the star?"

A shudder lingered in my voice as I followed her while she stormed through bracken and onwards toward the edge of the forest. Einya spun around, braids beating against her face as she whirled to face me.

"If Parlenta comes here, what then?" she spat.

"What?"

"Did you think they would just leave us? Do you think they won't find out from Bri that there's a star here? They're going to torture him, Tollska, if they haven't already. I can't know what they are doing. He isn't alright and if they come here, then I need some way to defend us. I might need some way to free him. Do you think I can do any of that without the star?"

"I … hadn't … if they come here and there's no star, there's nothing for them."

"They will check and take anything—anyone—linked to the stars. Including you. Follow me, you haven't left the trees, and I have looked beyond them."

"I'm … still linked?"

She twisted around wordlessly, striding through ferns and foliage as I scampered after her for what seemed like a long and silent hour until we reached the edge of the canopy. There, Einya turned, and wrapped one arm around my shoulders and gently squeezed. With her free hand, she raised one finger and pointed to the horizon—but she didn't need to.

In the distance, pillars of smoke towered to the sky where once pillars of stone stood. The burning of everything I once knew.

"I … didn't think it would come to this," I said, tearing one hand through my tousled hair. "Why do you think they will come here?"

"Trees burn easier than stone. We're the last easy pickings."

"So, what does that mean?" I whispered, clutching her closer to me. I already knew.

"What do you think? We have to do something so he can be free, so Bri has somewhere to come at the end of it all."

"That's what you've been looking into the stars for? To see if you can find him?"

Head resting against mine, a simple nod was her only response. Cramps spasmed down my arms and my throat tensed, breath pulsing out my lungs in short rasps. In that moment, it all came crashing down on me. I'd given her an impossible choice: abandon Bri or face my anger at her use of the stars.

VI
Pacts And Providence

~ TOLLSKA ~

The next morning, grey clouds shrouded the entrance to the forest as I sat at the edge of the trees, looking out across the lush fields beyond the woodland border. Rubbing the back of my neck, watching the plumes of smoke of my old home, my thoughts froze one after the other. I'd spent so much time hiding in the forest from the stars, I'd forgotten to look outwards. Forgotten to understand the wider world. *No more,* I swore.

Einya was somewhere behind me, clustered with Breyncda and a few others, debating the usage of the stars and what should be done next.

It was the rags I noticed first, clinging—soaked—around a strange figure who limped along the path toward the forest. Heaving myself up, a pattering of heartbeats trembled in my chest. There was something *wrong* about this creature. Like he walked how he thought a person should, but something about it did not flow naturally.

"Einya," I called over my shoulder. "Someone approaches."

She didn't listen, or even see me. The figure moved preternaturally fast, despite the strange limp, and only moments passed before the figure stood before the gate into the trees with an expectant look.

"Is the hospitality of Aisren absent these days?" the figure asked in a sibilant, smooth voice.

A guard at the forest gateway did not move as I shuffled closer.

"I do not recognise you," the first guard said, flinching almost.

"Do not recognise Warneraii?" the figure said. "I suppose this outfit is very different to others I have worn."

"I do. Let them in," the second guard said. "Warneraii will bring tidings."

"Warneraii always does," the strange figure said. "For good or ill."

I flinched backward, hovering in the shadows of the gateway trees as the doorway sprung open and the ragged figure of Warneraii stepped inside. A strange glow pulsed from them, and I knew where I'd seen that before. I tried to step into the deeper canopy, but bright eyes flicked straight to me.

"You are star-touched," Warneraii said. "Come out here."

"No, I'm not," I said, quickly shaking my head.

"I can smell it on you. Smell our blood."

"Who are you?" I spat. "You do not incentivise me coming out, whoever you are."

"I am a star."

Staggering backward a few paces, my heart hammered in my chest again. *How?*

"You are a person …"

"Not entirely, I wear a person much like the stars began to wear you …"

"How do you know that?" I said, stepping out but raising one hand to keep the strange figure at a distance. "The last star in a person I saw was a feral beast …"

"I see all, and I am different. I have control."

My head thrummed with a million more questions, but at that point, Breyneda and Einya stepped up close. Einya snaked one hand into mine and started to pull me away. I held resolute.

"No, I need to understand …"

"There will be a time for that," Warneraii said, before turning to Breyneda. "Lady of the forest, looks like it is time for us to plan again."

"Indeed. A drowned sailor this time?"

"It was all I could find, but preferable to the girl lost at sea I had once before. She was slow to move about with."

"What is it this time?" Breyneda sighed.

Einya stepped forward, still clinging to me.

"What is happening?" she said, echoing the question burning on my lips.

"Ah, allow me to properly explain myself," Warneraii said, bowing awkwardly and flicking wet from the matted curls upon their borrowed head. Black-blue lips, bruised by suffocation, split into a grin that sent a shudder through every scrap of me. "I am a sunken star, watching and trying to steer you all away from disaster. I wear the bodies of those who sink into the waves."

"Warneraii is how we knew of what happened in Gemynd first off," Breyneda said. "Shall we come inside? Settle somewhere?"

Several surreal moments later, we all sat cross-legged in a grove, Einya having walked confidently ahead while I shuffled behind her. Warneraii's skin distended, damp and swollen, as they'd sat down. The body's knees threatened to cut through the weakened flesh, and I couldn't tug my eyes away. It was better than looking at the waterlogged, bulging eyes within the creature's skull.

"Welcome back, Warneraii. Tell me what it is that snares you out of the sunken deeps," Breyneda said.

"One action of those here," Warneraii rasped, swollen tongue revealed with each bit of speech. "You."

The strange, corpse-like figure raised an emaciated finger and jabbed it toward Einya, causing a horror to crumble any reserve I had left. Einya held me tight as I tried to flinch away.

"What do you mean?" she said, words clipped.

"You and your brother go too far. He has drunk too much of my siblings' blood, and you use it to commune with him using this star. I know about the fox he used to survive. When does this end?"

"My brother is in danger; the fox keeps him alive. I am trying to save him. If you care for your siblings, then you must understand my concern."

An awkward silence, fraying the peace of the woodland, tore at me.

"Wait," I said. "You come here, having taken someone's body, and you lecture us about the use of the stars. What about your use of us?"

"Tols …" Einya said, nails digging into my hand.

Breyneda watched me intently, a small smile tugging at her lips.

"I am the watcher in the waves, the sea-star of many millennia. I do not need to answer to you," Warneraii chimed.

"Then do not expect me to listen," I spat. "I have been buffeted by the stars enough."

Those blotchy lips spread uncomfortably broadly again. "I do not have to expect you to listen. I will make you see."

Warneraii reached out, slender, bone-like fingers reaching for me.

"Tols … wait, let's not do anything rash," Einya rasped, reaching one hand out between us. "What disaster? You spoke of one, Warnerraii. What disaster?"

Breyneda watched, no words springing from her lips.

"One where the overuse of the stars will break apart what little is left of this place. We are fading, but will not fade without a spark that will tear all you know asunder. I do not wish to see the greed of this place destroy what's left of my siblings."

"Then what do we do?" I rasped.

"What do you think?" Breyneda said, at last, turning to me. "Return them to where they came from."

"Make it so nobody can use them. That's what you mean, isn't it?"

"Tols …" Einya whispered, clenching my hand and tugging me away.

"What? It would end things. End it all. There would be freedom and no fear of the stars."

"How do you think this would go?" Einya whispered. "They require our blood to mingle with theirs to do anything. That's how Warneraii takes their bodies, it seems, and that's how you were bound to the stars. To do enough to get them to leave. What would that take?"

"I can help you there …" Warneraii said. "In fact, it is my ultimatum. I will help you remove the stars so my brethren are not used in your petty politics, and in return, I will take any remaining residue of the star-beasts from your home."

At last, a way for the stars to leave …

"I agree."

"Tols, this isn't just for you to agree. We need to be careful …"

"What about this place? This safe haven from all the conflict, the place we have made home," Einya babbled.

"You are reluctant to lose the stars," I snapped, tugging my hand away from Einya.

"It is done then," Breyneda said.

"You agree too?" I whispered.

"I have learnt to listen to Warneraii. If this is what he says will work, we will see it done. Aisren's protection from the stars was ever a borrowed thing. We could not expect to keep it forever."

"And maybe one day we humans should fare on our own."

Einya pinched her lips together, gripping my head tightly. One little nod was all she gave, but her hitched breathed belayed a pool of deeper concerns when I glanced over.

"Then let us begin … I will guide your brother to free himself."

"What will he have to do?" Einya rasped.

"Do you want him free, or not? Trust Warneraii, like your friend Breyneda does," the star said, eyes bright.

"What will you do?"

"He has no other choice but to listen to me and free the stars. He will free himself if he does."

Einya and I exchanged a glance, her fingers digging deeply into my hand. At least Bri would be free. At least we would all be free.

An hour later, we stood with the star, or rather they did. I loitered at the edge of the glade, looking up through the gap in the canopy of trees where the star had fallen through into the forest many years ago. Grey clouds shrouded the sky from constellations and, for that, gratitude burnt in my heart even as a light rain pattered onto the leaves. The scent of wet fungus, mouldering leaves and dew blended into a fresh petrichor that soothed my nerves and reminded me of the forests on the edge of Rask. Maybe one day I'd return there when the stars were gone, and none of this would linger over them anymore. I could sit again by the river where we burnt my mother's bower and remember better times.

Einya, Breyneda and Warneraii stood in a triangle next to the star. The conversation had lingered on for hours, and while Einya had invited me to join it, she hadn't looked surprised when I shook my head. It was taking too long. I wanted to grip her by the shoulders and shake her—hadn't she seen what the stars had done to me, and now Bri? To Luskena? To all of our home? And yet, destroying them wasn't an option to her.

"What is happening?" I called.

Einya turned, her braided hair tussled from where she had run her hand over it repeatedly.

"Warneraii wants to use the connection to Bri via the fox to coax Bri into freeing the stars."

"Freeing the stars, how?"

"Sending them home."

"Sounds good to me …"

Einya's lip curled.

"But Bri will be once again manipulated. Can his mind take it?"

"It has so far …" Warneraii said.

An idea crept over me.

"Use Luskena. Talk to him via Luskena. She's said she can speak to him in the shadows. Maybe with Warrneraii she can speak to him directly? Maybe that will help him, rather than jolt him further."

"This is so. I could do this." The star simply nodded, but the flesh on the body's neck bulged as they did.

"How do you know?" Einya said. "Do you guarantee my brother will be his own person, free, after your guidance? Can you be sure you can even find Luskena to do this?"

"I can feel them all in the stars. They are all there—anyone who has ever tasted or blood-linked with them. Even you. Even Tollska. I can do this, but in exchange I want my own freedom."

I shuddered, digging my fingernails into the bark of a nearby tree. I couldn't be that person, had to be more than the shadow of the star-touch.

"Fine …" Einya said, turning to Warneraii. "We use Luskena."

"It is the right choice, a timeless choice and more potent than you know."

"There is no right choice here," I spat. "Just the least wrong one."

"As you wish it."

I turned to leave. A soft hand gripped my wrist—pulling me way.

"Tols, I'm sorry," Einya whispered, her voice low and husky.

I turned back, unable to help myself amid my desire, embers burning in her eyes for me. Desperate to know that I still counted more to her than the stars. She raised one finger, brushing it over my cheek bone as I stepped closer. Our bodies, contoured together, felt more natural than any of the glistening stars. I resisted pressing in closer as I wanted to.

"You have to focus." I swallowed, a thick lump in my throat. "Do what you need to, fulfil this pact and then let's leave. Let's be *us* again, away from all this."

"I fear there will be more steps."

"What do you mean?"

"Luskena tells Bri what to do, but what then?"

"We hope."

"And if he doesn't, or cannot, do it? Cannot free the stars?"

"Then maybe this Warneraii will do more. Do you trust this star?" I said, looking up at her.

"Not entirely, but Breyneda does. And they are neutral, so whatever he chooses must be for a general aim of improving things."

I bit my lip.

"Is it neutral? I believe it chases what the stars want, and nothing more."

"Then hope is indeed all we have," Einya sighed.

"And trust. Trust in Bri, and his madcap plan."

"Like all of his foolish plans," Einya grinned.

"I'm glad you still remember how to smile. Go on then," I whispered, stroking her cheek. "Get this done and then run away with me."

Her smile, subtle, only raised one side of her lips—but it was enough.

"Where will we go?"

"Anywhere. Home? But a home without the stars."

"Home is where you tread, Tols. I will be back," she mumbled, lifting my hand to her soft lips and kissing it gently.

I watched her trudge back into the glade with the star, pulling out a dagger and readying herself to reach out to Bri. The three of them knelt, Warneraii behind Einya with their mottled lips grazing her ear as he instructed her on what to do.

I flinched, almost lurching forward as Einya opened the gash on her arm, calling Bri's name and pulling forth the connection once again. I hurried back into the thicker tree line with bile burning in my throat. One day we must be free, but for now I thought of Bri and hoped that this plan would help him—despite the torrent of doubts surging tidally through my stormy thoughts.

~ BRI~

Something was happening, changing and writhing. My paw, pressed to the undulating star-rock, spiked with heat as I yelped and leapt back. The belt disintegrated. I was *free*. My nose twitched at a familiar scent: some kind of flower mingled with the stench of too many people in a bar. Then the voice pulsed around the cavern, echoing. It was different—not just the familiar female voice, but something metallic laced in with it.

"Go, Bri, get out of here."

My four legs quivered, knees bending against my will as I sagged to the floor.

"Get up," the voice spat. "Stop using the stars and get them out of Gemynd. I hold you to this task."

How?

It was a thought, only, yet somehow the voice answered me. The sibilant words tolled, bell like, wakening me with a start. Despite the darkness of night, it was like a curtain had been torn from its railing, spilling light into my eyes and banishing all my muddled confusion.

"I will show you how. Do as I bid. Wait for Warneraii … now run."

"Listen and do as he bids. Please," a second voice said. *Familiar. Luskena?*

Not needing to be told twice, I scampered from the place—running blindly into the night, myself and Quandary—as one for what would be the last time.

VII
Time Of Choices

~ BRI ~

"Bri …" a voice mumbled, gnarled fingers pressing to my cheek. "Wake up."

A figure in a cave, blood-soaking its skin. A time of choices.

"The time of three is approaching …" My lips formed the words, though it didn't feel like they were mine. "Get to the stars."

"Bri …" Prethi was shouting, far too close, his weight heavy beside me on the bed. One hand clutched mine, and the other gripped my shoulder, shaking it lightly.

"Where am I?"

"Where you were before, but back now … you'd faded somehow."

Prising my eyes open, light refracted in my vision as both Prethi and Paska swam into view.

"Something is coming …" I rasped.

"You need to rest."

"No … something is coming, and it is angry. It has a plan, and the queen expects me"

"Angry?" Prethi said, stepping forward. "In all our years causing mischief, I've never seen you this worried. Bri … the queen is not here."

"She will come, and I haven't got her the star-blood."

"Bri …"

Pressing myself up on trembling hands, I paused. A heavy weight lay slumped over my belly, russet fur quivering.

"Quandary …" I whispered, brushing one quivering hand through his fur. Clumps of it stuck to my fingers in crimson clots. My lower lip trembled as I gathered him into my arms. "What happened to you?"

"He ran back in here, Bri, bleeding everywhere. He charged toward you and suddenly you gasped and returned. What is happening?"

"He saved me from what I did to myself. I see it clearly now … I am lost with the stars in the very way I'd always hated, and he tried to save me."

"Why?"

"I don't know, but we're connected somehow."

"You're back now," Prethi said, still sitting gently on the side of the rickety bed. Both he and Paska watched me intently. "That's all that matters."

"Am I? And at what cost? He has paid the price for my vanity."

Quandary's little body trembled again then, and my heart clenched as if gripped within a steel gauntlet.

"Bri, you can't have known …"

"I should have. All along I should have."

"Bri, stop this. Would Luskena thank you for moping?" Paska tutted, swatting my cheek where dribbles of tears tumbled down.

I glared up at her, even as my hand brushed through Quandary's matted fur.

"Luskena and Quandary both paid prices for my meddling. I know understand what I must do. I know where Pearth is. I can end this once and for all."

"What are you going to do, Bri?"

"Do what I should have done a long time ago, Prethi. I'm going to kill her for what she has done to this place."

A hissing sound burst from Paska. Her grin in the shadows of the room as she stepped back.

"Do it but do it for you—do it for *us*. Not because the queen told you to," was all she said, before stepping from the room.

"Bri, are you sure?" Prethi muttered, shuffling a bit closer to me on the bed and glancing at the bleeding fox.

"Of course," I said, setting my jaw like steel and wrapping my arms around myself. "She hurt Einya, destroyed this place, almost turned Tollska into a star beast and then used me—Quandary—to try to defend herself and now I don't know whether the fox who saved me will survive. What good is there in her?"

"You're probably right, Bri," Prethi said, taking my hand and squeezing tightly. "Remember there is good in you, and I don't want that to go out. Don't become a killer."

"All goodness will snuff out if I leave this place to suffer under her rule."

"Hate is not you. You … are loved. I mean people love you. Others, I mean."

"You have too much faith in me. I've failed the ones who have loved me."

Prethi's silence stung, contorting in me as I blinked rapidly and ran one hand through my blood-crusted hair. *Was this the right path?*

"Prethi, I am only trying to save what I can … however I can."

"Then let's get you well again," he said, reaching for bread at the side table.

Sometime later, Paska returned with a broth and the pair of them nagged, teased, and cajoled me into eating even when my weak body failed and hot soup dribbled down my pallid chin.

✩ ✩ ✩

Claws plunged into me in my dreams for days. Luskena's bright eyes, dulled into tumultuous bloody storms, glared at me as she dug her hands deep into my guts and howled as she ripped them out. This time, someone watched—a distended face, waterlogged skin and dull eyes glossed over with a hollow distant gaze.

As I jerked out of my sleep, howling for the tenth day running, I knew: *it is here.*

"Prethi, I need to find her."

"You've tried to get up several days running. You need to rest," Prethi said, pressing me back down again.

"No. Now it is different. Bring me the stick and my blade. I won't take no for an answer. I have to find her."

"Or what, Bri?"

"A star is coming …"

"What?"

"A different star, from a different place. I don't understand, but I know this: he will hold me to account for what I have done. My day of judgement looms, and I won't go into it passively."

"I don't understand …" Prethi mumbled, pressing the splintered wooden stick into my hand.

Quandary whimpered a little in his rest next to me. We had curled up together this week past: neither of us healed, neither of us whole.

"Sorry little fox, it's time I make this right. I'll get you some star-blood—make you right again."

"How can you know that's what he needs?"

"I can't, just I have nothing else to try. He has spent himself to save me. Now help me up."

Prethi's arms gripped me tightly, not relenting at all as he lifted me out of the bed. When I whimpered, he looked sideways at me muttering: "This is what you wanted".

I smirked and kept trying to shift my weight off the bed and onto my groaning legs.

"When did you become so rough?" I said.

"When did you become so biddable?"

"We all change, I guess."

Before we left, I scooped up the trembling body of Quandary. A terrible pull tore at my heart: a fraying thread inside me, finally tugging free.

"I can't leave him," I said, my voice cracking.

"You can't take him either."

"I have to ... need save him," I stammered, looking around at was around me. "Rip the sheet up, tie him to me."

"You can't be serious ..."

"I'm perfectly sure."

Prethi shook his head, glancing up at me as he ripped the sheet into a roughly constructed papoose and wrapped my fox saviour within it about my chest.

"I hope you know what you're doing," he said, eyes cast down at my feet even though his hand hovered at my elbow.

I just nodded. It would be difficult, but I had to find a way.

Before we left, Paska returned with harsh words about making sure I didn't get myself killed—softened only by a gentle smile. Her wrinkled hands brushed over my arm, and she gently embraced me around where Quandary nestled against me. The little fox gekkered slightly, snuffling his snout weakly against my body.

"Thank you for everything, Paska," I whispered. "Can I ask you to do one more thing?"

She pulled away, raising one eyebrow.

"After saving your sorry self from a path of destruction, entirely of your own making, you expect me to help again? Do you hear this, Prethi?"

"I hear his delusion, loud and clear," Prethi muttered, but both of them were grinning.

"Tell the queen I have the stars, tell her I have Pearth, and I will give them to her. Bring her to the star cave."

"What?" Prethi said, stepping forward and pulling me around. "You have none of those."

"How else to we get her here?"

"She will bring her soldiers."

"And they will fight, and die most likely, to the beasts."

Prethi shook his head, his hand tightening into a fist at his side. "That is a fool's plan."

"That's the only type of plan I have, so you should be used to that by now," I said, a pulse of relief at Prethi's smirk that accompanied his eye roll.

"I'll do it, but you better be ready. She'll come quickly."

"Then we best go."

"Bri?" Paska said.

"Yes?"

"It's good to have you back, mad plans and all," she said, swatting me on the back of the head.

"Thank you," I rasped, and hobbled over for a final embrace.

"Come back."

"I'll try."

"This is for you," Paska said, digging the small box out of her pocket. *The silver ring.*

A deep breath of fresh *free* air, the first in months, filled my lungs as I ran my hand over the box.

"Keep it for me? Give it to me if I get back."

"*When* you get back", she said, tutting and turning. "Make it quick."

Turning to leave, I managed a few steps at a time with Prethi one side and the stick on the other. At the door of the crumbling hut, I stumbled as the scent of burning tore at the inside of my nose. I'd seen it before, but not fully as myself. A gripping horror stabbed at my heart at my once pristine home, now stained in offal, blood, and grime. I rubbed one of Quandary's ears absently, his soft fur soothing against my worn fingers.

"How do we come back from this?" I rasped.

"You kill Pearth, remember? If you're sure that's what you want …"

"*Mmm.*"

"You could just leave. We could leave and live a free life somewhere far away …"

"It is too late for that."

"Is it? Does it have to be?"

Despite my resolute words, a churning tide of uncertainty washed over me as step by step we limped toward the cave where the star-rock dwelt. If the beasts found us … I shoved the thought away. What would I even do when we got to the star?

"What is your plan, Bri?" Prethi mumbled, as if reading my uncertainty or feeling the tension in my body when he'd said I'd kill Pearth. "Bring the queen, and then what?"

"Kill the Parlentan queen and destroy the stars. It is the only way to stop the Parlentans getting the stars ..." I swallowed, eyes darting to the floor. Don't look into his eyes. Don't think about her glittering eyes and parted lips. An outstretched hand, clad with rings and shimmering with Astamitra ready for me to lick straight from her flesh. I shook my head, banishing the tempting thoughts.

"How? You're not a killer; how are you going to do this?"

"Someone is coming. They will help."

"Who? You speak in riddles."

"I don't know, Prethi, but someone ... they spoke to me ... and I will know them by their drowned complexion. Their name is Warneraii. That is all I can tell you, and I don't even know that it's true or imagined."

I ignored his uncertain glare from Prethi and stumbled further into the street. Grateful for the shadows of night to hide the uncertain frown on my brow, as well as to conceal our journey from any lingering beasts. We slowly shuffled through alleys, pausing often. Thankful for our misspent youths hiding in these passages from responsibility of rank, we paused often in entrances to cellars and eating morsels Prethi had luckily thought to bring.

"I'm going to sit for a while; my legs are quivering."

"You should eat more."

"I am trying to," I said, feeling the tightness of my stomach as I forced down the smallest scrap of preserved meat and felt like I'd eaten a whole roast chicken. "I feel like something is in my stomach, clawing its way up."

My eyes stretched wide as I shuddered. *Long talons, star-beasts screeching.*

"Come on Bri, let me help you sit," Prethi said, hefting one arm underneath me and lifting me up. "I'll help you. I'll be here all the time you need, if you'll let me.

"I've got to do this myself, Prethi. You've done so much."

"Because I care, and you would do the same for me. Have done the same for me, protecting me all this life from insignificance. Giving me a home, when I had nothing else ..."

"I know, and I want you with me, but I'm still stubborn," I said, smirking, clutching my ribs with my spare hand. A small sputter of laughter threatened to split them open where my stomach churned.

Balancing myself, weight pressed through the stick, I lowered myself down and dropped with a thump to the slick steps up to a boarded-up house. The properties here were bigger, and though it was hard to recognise the streets, so battered and strewn with bodies that they were. It told me one thing: we were getting close.

Despite the thick smog over the city, searing light strained my gaze and my eyes flickered shut. My hair, slick and matted against the back of my head as I leant back and rested it against the wooden slats over the door, made me itch to wash it. When was the last time I had? I was sure my hair must be as matted as Quandary's fur. Breath hitched in my throat, my eyes sagging shut. Digging my dirty fingernails into the side of my leg didn't make the sensation fade. My last thought before a rumbling sleep claimed me was of the clatter of the stick falling from my hand when I let it go and instead clutched the fox close to me.

Something kicked my foot.

"Bri, wake up," Prethi hissed, crouched inches from my face.

"What is it?" I mumbled, groggy, reaching one hand to twine in Prethi's tattered doublet. I clung on too tightly, eyes wide, as my hand ached with the grip.

"I'm here, it's alright … but something is watching us."

"One of the beasts?"

"I don't know."

"Let's move."

Silently, and as efficiently as we could manage, Prethi heaved me from the steps and when I was able to shuffle on with the help of the stick, he drew a blade. We advanced like that, quietly, Prethi's back to mine and the tap of the stick and the rasping of my voice being the only sounds we couldn't avoid. Darkness trickled down from the sky and into the streets. Even so a shadow lurched after us, observing us from every crack and nook in the damaged buildings around us.

"There it is," I said, dragging Prethi's gaze forward and aware of the shadows.

"The Astrologers' Tower?"

"Yes, at last."

It couldn't have been long but it felt like hours since Prethi had lifted me from the steps. The square was open. Too open. Any step into it, and whichever beasts lingered here would surely see us. A shiver coursed through me, seeing the cart I'd been strapped to when Quandary and I were one. Now I would have to face it alone. My fingers tightened around the stick. *There must be a way.*

"Prethi …"

"What?"

"Can you check whether anything waits around the corner? Don't want it to chase up behind us when we go for the tower."

He nodded, stepping brusquely around the corner to check the shadows with blade raised. I took the snatched moment and did the only hare-brained thing I could think would work—dug the final vial of star-blood from my robe and glugged down the dregs. The fizzle of energy wasn't much, but it was enough.

"Come on Prethi, I think I've got one run in me. Let's do it."

"You think you can run?" he scoffed, returning.

"Trust me."

"Bri ... have you ...?"

I looked at him, and we shared no words—just a look of aching regret. We took off, stick tapping faster now as we bounded clumsily across the square. Hairs prickled on the back of my neck, and I pounded on despite my cracking, tender knees quivering with each step. The fissure, just big enough to hurl ourselves through, couldn't come soon enough as a howl erupted nearby.

"Any faster, Bri?"

"Not really."

Foolishly, I glanced back and saw the writhing form of a star beast scrabbling out of a nearby window. Beyond, a strange figure stood—mottled lips, tangled hair and torn robes flowing around him in the wind. The beast didn't seem to notice, and I had no time to pause.

My voice screeched, grating in my ears. "Run, Prethi—go."

"No ..."

I tried to hobble faster, the last speck of star-blood bursting through me and sputtering out. Quandary gekkered, as if to warn me. Not daring to look behind me and, not needing to, I yelped as the howl ricocheted around the square again—it was getting closer. The thought of distended, bone-like claws shredding through my back washed through my mind and spurred me on the last way.

"Now," a voice shouted, and a rain of fire pattered down from the window of the tower. "Again."

"There are people in the tower ..." I said, rubbing my eyes as if to be sure I hadn't dreamt it.

Looking up, burning clusters of yarn and material lashed down onto the street. It was just what I needed to slow the beast as I reached the crack and Prethi heaved me through it, tugging us into a pile of limbs on the floor.

"Like old times, hiding from your family," Prethi muttered, giggling a little. "Is the beast following?"

"I don't think so. Let's say it isn't, or we'll forever look behind us."

"Good. One day, you'll stop getting me into trouble."

I couldn't help myself, a little laugh—a little of my old self—tinkled in the air. We were nose to nose, our arms and legs all tangled up and quite ridiculous. Quandary even stirred a little, gekkering happily in my arms and nestling against me.

"You are everything I need in this bizarre situation, Prethi. Know that always, in case I cannot tell you."

"You will always be able to tell me. Now get off and let's do whatever you came here to do."

I nodded.

"Are you sure about this? About this Warneraii?

"Einya told me somehow, or so I thought. I woke up knowing I had to come here and speak to this Warneraii. The time of three is coming."

"Bri … I'm worried you're not yourself. You're speaking as if in riddles."

Sighing, I ran one hand over my face. "I'll do what I can. I know I cannot wait for a fevered vision that may or may not be real. What else can I do? My brain is addled, and I struggle to put one foot before the other—let me just do my best."

"Then let's get inside, and you can tell me what this all means."

"If I knew, I would."

We scrambled upright and used the narrow corridor into the star cave to prop us up as we staggered into the central chamber. An icy tremble spasmed down my spine, footsteps stumbling so much that Prethi careened into the back of me. Quandary yelped in my arms, and I rubbed my hand over his head to calm him.

"What is it?"

"She's still here. Of course she is. She defends the people in the tower."

"Who?"

"Pearth—and I'm not ready."

"Then we will do this together, and maybe then you'll let me take you back to get better."

I nodded, not meeting his gaze, and we shuffled forward into the cavern where the word-weaves of fate and vengeance would at last be answered.

"I know you're there."

The words came, cold and sad. Her lone figure turned, silhouetted against the torch-lit star.

"Say nothing," Prethi whispered. "Go back. Let me do this."

"No …" I hissed, gripping his wrist with one hand. "You've done enough."

"And I will continue to, until the day when I see you back to yourself and your eyes are no longer grey and bloodshot with a crave for star-blood."

"What are you colluding about?" Pearth said, circling toward us as she drew a blade. "Muttering like children in the shadows, just like when you were children."

I stepped forward, letting the stick fall away from my grasp and instead tugging at Prethi's dagger until it came loose from the sheath in his belt. Wrapping my free arm around Quandary, I protected the fox from her.

"You did all this," I growled, a burning tide of anger surging from my stomach and forking my tongue with fierce words.

"I know," she said. "And I hang on with only scraps of strength as I try to fix this."

"Then pay for it. Pay for what you did to Luskena, to Einya, to Tollska."

I lurched forward, blade raised, ready for blood to pulse over it and cover my hands as I shielded Quandary with my other arm. My cousin scowled back, running one hand through her tangled hair as she turned to me.

"I pay every day, in the death of all those around me. All I did, I did to try keep Gemynd safe. I have the last of our people to keep alive."

"And where are they now? The people you keep safe."

"They are barricaded in the tower above us, surviving on scraps. We are running out of time."

"By yourself?" Prethi said.

"Then at least it would see an end for me. When the beasts come back to the stars, I can try to end this. You could help us, instead of hating me for trying me best."

Her words took the wind from my venomous words, but I pressed the blade to her chest all the same.

"I'm going to give you to the Parlentan queen," I hissed.

"What?" Prethi gasped behind me. "I thought that …"

"I vowed to do so, and she will give me more star-blood for you. Then you will never use the stars for ill again."

"You are working for their queen," Pearth said, words dead and hollow. "Traitor."

"No ... I am working to do what will cause you the greatest pain. Working to stop you controlling Gemynd and Rask."

"Whether you realise it, or not, you are working for her. I wish you and her all the luck getting past the beasts."

"The beasts you made ... what you made Luskena into."

Prethi's fingers gripped my shoulder, trying to steer me away.

"Don't do this, Bri ... you can't take more star-blood. I know you want vengeance, but this doesn't seem to be about that."

"Listen to him, Bri. We were cousins once, and while I welcome death—this isn't you."

"You are wrong. Prethi, trust me. Please ... I need it to end this."

I thrust the dagger, but it would not budge. A searing light burst through the cave. I covered my eyes with my spare hand.

"This isn't the answer," a new, ice-laced voice said. "I told you to wait."

"Bri ..." Prethi called, trying to lurch toward me where the new figure stood—gripping my arm and stopping the plunge of the blade into my cousin's heart. As the light faded, dead eyes stared at me, pupils dulled in colour and a deep sadness permeating every scrap of grey within them. Tingling horror swept over my skin as I looked into those muted eyes. I forced it down.

"How did you get here? Can't you see I'm busy?"

"Your sister said you'd be cheeky to the last."

"You were with Einya?" I croaked, voice hitching in my throat. "Is she alright?"

The creature's grin spread wide. His breath—if it could be called that—swathed me in a rotten yet sweet stench. *Just like Astamitra.*

Licking my lips, dagger sagging away from Pearth's heart, I leant toward this newcomer.

"You have not worked it out. I am Warneraii," the figure whispered, soft and luring. Enough to make me turn full from my cousin.

"You told me to wait ..."

"And here I am," Warneraii said, reaching a clammy hand up and gripping my fingers where they held the dagger. "Come."

"How did you get here?"

"Through the star, of course. Now let us begin."

"Bri ... I cannot move," Prethi whispered. "What is this?"

"The time and gift of three," Warneraii said, before I could say anything. "And this is just the first part."

The Time of Three

THREE SACRIFICES

Blood Reclaimed

Lives Lost

Lives Found

VIII
The First

~ BRI ~

"Release us," Pearth growled.

I pressed the dagger to her chest, but my grip slackened on the hilt. The three of us stood in a triangle, Warneraii smiling as he circled us.

"Yes, you will do. I see you have the fox, good."

"You leave him out of this," I spat, tightening my grip around Quandary as the fox buried his head into the nook of my arm.

"For now, if you wish."

A loop of starlight, stretched on the floor, held us in place. Running my spare hand along its gossamer edge, I hissed and dragged my hand back close to my chest. Looking down, singed brown flesh tingled on my fingertips—still burning somehow.

"Why do you hold us here?" I muttered, before sucking the tips of my fingers and looking sideways at Warneraii. *What choice did I have?*

"There is something you must do for me. You two who claim to be cousins—

"We do not claim to be cousins," Pearth said. "No cousin of mine holds a blade to my chest."

"No more of this. You will do as I bid. I can give you another way. I have travelled here from Einya Arden."

"My sister sent you ..." I gasped, hand dropping to my side, burning fingers forgotten.

"Yes, to have you help me."

"Why?" Prethi said. "You have imprisoned us and given us no incentive to help you."

"How did you get past the Parlentans?"

"I am starlight and dust," Warneraii said. "I will give you what each of you wants. I will get these Parlentans gone from your home."

"Why has she sent you?" I hissed. "I had this under control."

"Did you?"

"Yes," Pearth said. "Did you? As far as I can tell, everything you have done has made it worse."

Warneraii's water-crinkled hand suddenly brushed up the side of my neck and traced over my lips. The dusky stench of Astamitra lingered on his flesh, too, and I had to tense every part of me to hold myself from running my tongue over his fingers.

"Control is something you are barely gripping on to, Briarth. I can feel you, craving the stars with each breath."

"Hypocrite," Pearth spat.

"I did what I had to," I whispered, casting my eyes down to the ground. "Just like you."

The star held up an arm to silence us.

"You use the blood of my people to your own ends. You both did. Now you will make amends."

"So, what do you want?" Prethi said. "How do we end this?"

"Return my people to the skies before they fade forever."

"How does this give us what we want?" I growled. "I *need* the stars."

"This is the pact I have agreed with your sister. You will do this here, and she will do this in the forest. There will be nothing for Parlenta to claim. Your war will be done."

Teeth bared as Warneraii looked into my eyes and I growled at him, fox like.

"Why should we do this?"

"This is how you get free from all this. The war will be done, but vengeance won't be."

The drowned star leant forward, a single breath grazing my ear as he whispered.

"This is only the beginning. Remember your plan. There is someone who wants to talk to you."

A jerking movement coursed through me: I could move again. One precious thought, greater than all the urges I felt to thrust the dagger back through Pearth's heart and claim more star-blood from the queen ... *the fox*. The etching stung in my leg where I'd dug the shape in with a sharp edge all that time back. *Kill the queen. Save the fox.* How could I have forgotten?

Starlight swam through the cavern, Warneraii's hand placed over my eyes and their sweet breath pulsed down my lungs. Distantly, Prethi's voiced shouted my name.

"How did you survive all this?" Warneraii said. "Our blood addles humans' minds …"

"The fox helped me, took the star into him. Saved me," I croaked.

"Or perhaps he was a star all along. Did you think of that?"

"Like you?"

"Like me. However so, I will have them back."

"No … he and I, we …"

My lips parted, and I ran my tongue over them, feeling sharp teeth— too sharp—as I did. The dagger in my hand clattered to the stones as I tilted my face upwards to be closer to Warneraii's star-scented fingers, where they rested on my face. *Perhaps this was the only way to heal Quandary.*

"Show me the fox," the star commanded.

"He is sick," I said, one hand tangling in Warneraii's fingers: clutching, desperate, pleading. "I want to help him. Help me save the fox, and I will listen to your asks."

"Listen to her, not me. Remember her."

From where Warneraii's fingers tingled on my skin, burning it like the border encircling us, light radiated. The cavern faded, my eyes blurring. Cold stone pressed to my back, but I saw no rock—just the brushing reeds of long grass grazing my knees as I stood in a sun-soaked field.

"Come join me, little troublemaker," she cried, her voice lyrically dancing over the notes of her words.

My lips parted as I stepped toward her, nestled in the grass that reached up above her head. Blades of green and amber brushed against my cheeks as I crouched down beside her.

"Is this real …" I rasped, one quivering hand reaching out to her. "I've spent so long in the darkness …"

"Then be with me at last in the light. Lie down."

I didn't need telling, my body aching and crumbling as I heaved myself down beside her.

"Are you just another vision?"

I flinched, as her hand rested on my chest where I lay amongst the long grass bristling against me softly and brushing my face.

"Breathe in, deeply. Remember what I smell like?"

"Ink and beer, usually."

"Can you smell it?"

"Yes," I rasped, chest heaving raggedly at the old, familiar wafting scent. "Though, there's something else. There's star about you too."

My eyes shot open, sunlight pulsing through them in the strange meadow where no wind blew and no blade of grass wavered.

"I am with the stars, Bri …"

I knew I was standing, but beneath me it felt as if the floor clattered away and I was cascading into nothingness.

"You died then. That's why I can hear you when I drink the stars, you're with."

"Yes."

"I worried you might still be one of them, just instead you'll be a beast …"

Her coarse fingers, rough as I remembered them, pressed to my lips.

"I have guided you. Couldn't you tell?"

A painful swallow, ragged in my throat, as I sat up and looked into her gaze.

"I don't know who I am anymore … I've lost it in star-blood, anguish, and vengeance."

"Then do what you must, and join me here …"

"Can I … touch your face? Are you …?"

She grabbed my fingers, with the rough and careless movements I remembered, tugging my singed hand up to her cheek and nestling into it.

"Answer your question?"

"Yes …"

"Einya helped me talk to you, and now Warneraii. The former wanted to help you, the latter wants to be free … between them, you can be free too."

"It is Quandary that has made me free."

"Quandary is spent."

"Don't say that," I croaked. "I'm going to save him."

"Save him by saving yourself. He took the star-blood from you, took your hurt away. Don't cheapen that. I can see the colour of your eyes again. He did that."

"I worried they would never come back …"

Luskena's laugh, musical, as she leant forward and put a finger at either side of my mouth—raising my lips into a smile before my muscles took over and I grinned widely.

"Of course, only I can do this for you. I'll bring back your mirth too," she said.

"What now?" I whispered, shuffling closer and seeing a tinge of concern flicker through her eyes as her brow creased together.

"End this."

"How?"

"Work with this Warneraii, he has sent my voice to you since he rose from the waves."

"I can't. I can't trust anyone in Gemynd, except Prethi and Paska."

"Give the stars freedom and Warneraii will make it, so we are together again."

"But you're dead."

"He's a star, Bri. Haven't we seen enough of what they can do?"

"You trust in this?"

"I do … make that good enough for you if nothing else is," Luskena said, her fingers reaching up and brushing through my matted hair.

"I hope …"

"Don't hope. Believe," she said. "Now go. Kill the queen, free the stars. Release yourself from all of this and come back to me."

"I will. Luskena, I … I wish that with every scrap of me. Is peace possible, after all of this?"

Luskena gestured over the fields, I leant in, her warm skin blushing against mine. My hands tingled.

"Is this peace enough, Bri? Are there enough trees for you to hide behind and jump out at me, or rivers enough in the woodland beyond the cornfields that we might frolic in?"

"I suppose it will do." I grinned. "Stay with me … don't let me forget this. It was you, in the cell, I know that now. I couldn't have done any of this without you."

"There's a time where you will need to be without me, for us to be together again, my troublemaker."

"How can I find you …?"

Darkness shrouded in, the light fading as the tingling touch of Warneraii pulsed one last time with a shocking fissure tearing through me as the room returned around me. Leaning over where I lay, alone, I clutched my stomach claw like and wretched a glittering liquid over the stones. *I still had star-blood within me.*

Warneraii crouched over me, brushing hair out from between my lips as I wretched up more star-blood. Quandary placed a single paw on my chest, patting above my heart lightly as if to try to wake me.

"I'm alright, little fox. Settle down, save your energy."

"Free yourself," Warneraii said, looking down at both of us. "Free the fox too."

"I'm"—my words formed between gasps—"literally vomiting your relatives' blood. Why are you so calm?"

"Because one day you will return them to the stars once you have released them from this place."

Groaning, I sagged sideways, my arms quivering and giving way. Warneraii's caught me, held me upright against his body as my head lulled against his shoulder.

"Where are the others?" I sputtered, weakly trying to sit upright.

"They see what they need to see."

"Where are they?"

"Lying by the star."

My eyes adjusted in the darkness, two twitching figures lying by the looming rock lurked into view.

"Luskena thinks if I free the stars from the influence of this land, you will reunite us."

"She is right. That is what I offered her. She said you would do what was needed to make it happen."

"And what is that?"

"A ritual."

"Ritual?"

"To release the stars."

"Why do you need me for that?"

"Because you will spill the stars out of you as part of the ritual, you will return me and my brethren home. Now breathe, rest against me and soon you may discuss with your companions."

Leaning back, trembling against the strangely firm body of Warneraii, I shivered as damp fingers held my chin up.

"What are you doing?" I muttered, trying to prise myself away.

"Briarth ... you don't know, do you?"

"Know what?"

"You are choking. Choking on the stars."

"What ...?"

"Your body cannot take more. You are being sick, you are nauseous. You may have felt better when Quandary tried to save you, but ..."

"Be honest with me. Why are you helping me?"

"Because I don't know what will happen if you die with a star within you. My relative may never return home."

"And when the star leaves me?"

"I don't know that either. Spill blood from your veins, wretch up the star-blood and draw a circle on the ground. Your sister will do the rest."

"So, I am expendable," I said, shoulder caving in as I tried to hunch forward, but Warneraii's arms pulled me back upright.

"No. We can both help each other. Your sister will do her part, you will do yours, and I will do mine. You will be with Luskena again."

"You can make Luskena come back? And what do you mean about Einya? She isn't at risk?"

Warneraii looked away from me, eyes cast to the ground.

"Your sister will return their star, much as you will return this and take back all the star from the Queen of Parlenta. Begin the ritual, bring the queen here."

"I've already sent someone for the queen … I want her dead."

"Good. Then we are aligned. Now go to your companions. You will need them and do it quickly. I will tell you when to begin. Do not do it alone."

✵ ✵ ✵

Cold stone pressed against my hands as I crawled across the floor to the star, reaching trembling fingers out to Prethi's body where he lay. His eyes squirmed, fitful, beneath eyelids like slugs slowly undulating beneath leaves.

"Wake up," I croaked. "We need to do something."

I reached one hand down to tap the side of his face, kneeling so I didn't have to push all my weight through my trembling arm.

"Bri?" Prethi said, eyes slowly flickering open.

"Are you alright?"

"Never better," he said, a wide grinning pulling at his lips.

"What?" I said, leaning backward and rubbing my calloused fingers over my chin. "What do you mean?"

"I have a plan, and you will be free of the stars."

"Did … Warneraii tell you of the ritual?"

Prethi sat up, vigorous nods shaking his hair around his face.

"Yes, and how we'd get the stars back into the sky and you'll be free."

Sinking sharp teeth into my lip, I swiped my hand over my mouth. *Get rid of any lingered star dust.*

"Good, yes, free. I am glad you're on board with this."

"Why wouldn't I be?"

"No reason." I smiled, but I know the light didn't pierce my grey eyes. Prethi didn't miss it either. I felt his muscles tighten next to me.

"What is it, Bri? What aren't you saying?"

I swallowed, glancing away. *I couldn't tell him the truth … that I am still sick with the stars. That I didn't know what would happen when I did the ritual.*

"I just don't know if Pearth will help, that's all …" I muttered.

"We'll give her no other option."

"Prethi, wait …"

He'd rolled over, shaking my cousin awake. I glanced back toward Warneraii, who watched us from the shadows, water-bleached arms folded and distended lips pinched tightly. It was then, outside the caves, a howl sounded and the deep clawing scrapes of bone on stone echoed through the hollowed rock.

"What is going on?" Pearth snarled, rolling up onto the balls of her feet as she took in the scene and heard the screeches.

"We have a plan …" Prethi began, hands outstretched, ready to hold her back.

"The ritual? I know," she snapped. "This star has already shown me, shown me how if I work with you two, I can be free of you and free of the stars. How we can get rid of Parlenta once and for all."

Shock cascaded over me like ice, and my hand shot to my mouth. I turned, looking to find Warneraii. The shadow-shrouded figure had gone. At the door to the cavern, a sheen of light had burst over the gap—beasts scrabbling at the starlight but not able to burst through.

"What is it?" Prethi asked, the grin fading from his face.

"Warneraii has promised us each what we want," I said, swallowing down a searing bile of star-blood pulsing up my throat.

"What choice do we have?" Pearth spat.

"None at all. The beasts are here, and our only way to remove the stars is to do this ritual."

"That creature knew."

"Yes," I said. "It knew this was the only way you and I would work together."

"Then let's get it done, then I'll never have to look at you again."

"Pearth …" I rasped, "I wish it had been different…"

"Save it," she said, shoving one hand in my face and thrusting my head to one side. "I just want Parlenta gone, and these beasts gone, so we can rebuild."

"The beasts you had a hand in making," I said, my teeth chattering against each other with quivering anger. "Prethi, help me up."

I staggered to my feet; one arm looped over Prethi's shoulders as I shuffled after Pearth. Nails, too long now, sliced deep into my palm as I moved.

"You did this," I spat.

"To save our people."

"By damning others to death, by damning Luskena to death?"

"Stop!" Prethi yelled, a voice screeching in my ear. "Do you think we will have this window forever? Will the star hold the beasts away for long? We need to do this ritual … you both want the same thing!"

"He's right," Pearth said, chin tilted high as her hard eyes glared into my grey ones.

"If this wasn't …"

"Bri, stop it. We need to heal you, and you are stopping that. We need to do the ritual, rid you of the stars," he said, turning his head close to mine, where he held me up.

"Fine," I said, "if only to be done with *her* once and for all."

"Do you mean me, or the Parlentan queen? I know you do her bidding."

"Both, together."

"I don't care, as long as you help me get rid of the queen, dear *cousin.*"

"I am doing this for Luskena, and Quandary."

"Whatever reason you cling to, just let's get it done and then go our separate ways," Pearth growled, stepping into my space and towering over me. Once we were a similar height, but no longer. Defiant, I glared upward.

"Then let us be rid of the stars, before the queen even gets here."

"Ah good," Prethi muttered next to me, shifting his weight. A ghost of a smile traced his lips, and I could feel him fidgeting next to me. "So, how do we do it?"

"Take me as close as you can to the star," I croaked, smiling at the way he always had some joy in him. I would miss that. Would he still have that joy after everything I hadn't told him about happened, when the star-blood choked me further? When I spilt my star-soaked blood in a circle around the star and then died trying to kill the Parlentan queen or succumbed again to her? A heaving burst of bile lurched up my throat again at a single thought: *What would happen to the queen after the ritual? What would happen to Quandary?* Writhing on the floor, squealing as the star-blood melted through their pores … I pressed the thought away. It was time to be rid of all this.

IX
The Second

The week after Warneraii left to find Bri was a strange one in the forest. No more free festivities gracing the evenings, where gently burning oil lanterns hung from trees and dancing thrummed through the roots and mossy floors. Clear instructions had been left: to perform a ritual, letting the star leave. A few days, where Einya was scarce to be found, I found myself on the edge of the wood so as to be as far away from the star-rock as possible—digging words into fallen bark with a dagger.

Eventually, I'd made my own set of word stones, which I would cast onto the ground and try to divine a response for what was to come. The words fell in no meaningful pattern at all, and all I gleaned was my own gloomy thoughts had led me to carve words such as 'failure,' 'lost,' and 'death' on the bark and I concluded these told me nothing more than how pessimistic I had become.

No more of this. I had moped around and hidden away for long enough.

Forcing myself to wade through ferns and thickets to get to the star as quickly as possible, I brushed the undergrowth aside with sweeping strokes. I would find Einya, find out what was happening and help her end it if I could. The trees loomed longer over the path, shrouded as if tipping into the veil of night despite the high sun of midday beating down above the canopy.

In the grove, it seemed all the residents of Aisren had gathered. No wonder the rest of the forest felt empty.

"It can't be …" I heard myself say, a pounding susurration slicing through my mind. I thrust a hand out, grabbing a tree to steady myself.

In the glade, the vines were gone, and the ground was cleared. The stone, once clad in ivy and moss, was bare rock. The sun, pulsing in the sky, glared down—seeming ready to burn it to ash now it had no verdant protection. Einya knelt on the ground in a simple blue dress, a book in one arm and a stick in the other, carving symbols in the dirt. On the opposite side of the circle, Breyneda was doing the same. Similarly dressed, similarly dishevelled.

"Deep breath," I said, heaving air into my lungs. "This is for her."

I strode over the threshold, into the pulsing sun, trying to pick my way around runes carved into the earth until I stood by Einya's side. She looked up with eyes lined in blood, grey lids clouding the top of her gaze as she placed the book on her lap and raised her hand to shield herself from the sun beating down above me. Her skin, blistered and flaking, peeled away even as she looked at me. I crouched down, lifting my coat over her head to give her some shade.

"What are you doing, Einya? Where have you been? This is madness. I've not seen you in two days."

"I told you I need to prepare for the ritual Warneraii told us about. Breyneda says it takes days to carve the runes …"

"You need to look after yourself too. Since when did Breyneda make choices at the expense of your strength, and care for yourself?"

"Since she and Warneraii agreed this could save Bri … I have to save Bri," she said, voice cracking and grinding in her throat.

"You cannot save Bri unless you help yourself."

"It is too late for that … Warneraii is on the way to Gemynd. He could even be there by now. We need the ritual ready, so when Bri does his part, the star can leave him, and all the stars can go. This is the only way. This is what we *all* agreed to."

Einya looked up at me then, dull eyes writhing with blooded veins.

"I didn't realise it would be like this …"

"This is bigger than anything I've done. It will take a lot to give what's left of them back …" Einya stood with my help, brushing sweat from her flaking brow and batting away my hand when I tried to still her swaying body. "Please understand, Tols, a lot is being sacrificed here."

"What do you mean?" I said, words tumbling out. Not taking no for an answer, and settling my hand under her elbow to steady her while she stood, biting my lip until a trickle of blood ran over my quivering chin.

"The stars are going to leave. The heart of the forest will wither."

"What?" I said, eyes wide, almost pulling away from Einya.

Breyneda, equally flaking in skin and beaten by the sun, staggered over.

"This place was hidden by the star seeking to hide itself," she said. "Now, we will lose that."

"Then why did you agree?"

"Because," Breyneda rasped, "Warneraii has kept us safe for all these years, taught us how to live alongside the star in a way no-one listened to. They ask us for a single thing: to let them go home, now the use of the stars has gotten to be too much and gone too far. Is that not the least we can do?"

"And free Bri," Einya said, husky and almost silent.

"I want the stars to leave," I said, folding my free arm around myself. "But this, I do not understand. I thought it was as simple as just releasing the stars, but this is something more. You are giving your very strength up for this. How can you trust this creature?"

"Warneraii has never led us wrong before."

Glancing up, the glare of the sun seared my eyes until I had to look back. Had to confront this madness.

"What will it involve?" I whispered, reaching out and grasping one of Einya's blistered hands gently. She winced but said nothing as she gripped my fingers in return.

"It will entail the words in this book, said thrice," Einya said.

"Thrice?! You still sound like an Astrologer."

"Maybe on some level I am."

I dropped her hand, taking one step back from the star and stepping backward away from the clearing.

"I will look after her," Breyneda said, slowly following me.

"Will she need looking after, will you both be alright?"

"We don't know," Einya said, a strange look passing between the two of them.

"Very reassuring."

"Sometimes the stars are volatile, that is all," Breyneda said.

"All?" I ground out, teeth bared as Einya's arm snaked around my waist, tugging me away from the star.

"Tols, this is the last time. I promise."

"And if it goes wrong, it certainly will be."

"Please, trust me," she whispered, pulling me so close I could feel the tension in her muscles.

"I am trying to. I really am."

Chained to her glistening eyes, I watched her as the sun dipped behind a cloud. *Sweat, or tears?* I couldn't say, but my next words took me by surprise.

"I am leaving."

"What?" Einya rasped, her hand tugging me closer. "Please ..."

"I can't watch you do this."

"We're wed, we're one—you and I, against the world."

"You and I, and the stars."

"Don't make me choose."

"You make me choose, every day. You make me choose the stars, so I can still have you. You never left them behind. I will return when they are gone."

Her eyes definitely glistened, the bright sun bursting back from behind its hiding place and piercing the droplets of moisture pattering down her cheeks.

"I ... I fully understand. I had always dreaded this day. I hoped you would never say this, hope you wouldn't lay this condition on *us*."

Rubbing my hand over my neck before dropping it to my side, I stepped toward her, our foreheads lightly touching.

"My love for you is always and will be always, when this is done. I am doing this so you leave them, so you can be free."

"I became an astrologer for you ..."

"I know, and that's what makes this hardest of all. You don't need to be now, but you are. You still speak to them, and I see you gazing longingly when you think I'm not looking. I just can't watch the stars consume you any longer."

Her arms hung at her side as she sagged into a slouch, and I wrapped myself her around as I swallowed uncomfortably. *I should have spoken to her about this long ago.*

"I am doing this for you. For us, so you can not worry about me as you do what you have to do."

"I know, Tols, I know," she mumbled into my shoulder. "I'll be done with it, one way or another. I promise."

"When will you do the ritual?"

"Tomorrow, in the small hours," she whispered, her voice dim and hollow, as she lifted her head, placed her hand on my cheek, and brushed my brow with her crusted lips. "Until the stars fade, then."

"Until then. I'll meet you at the edge of the trees."

With that, I turned from the glade, feet snagging on vines as I stalked away with a gnawing terror writhing in my mind. At the edge of the forest I stopped, abrupt, thinking of my mother and how we'd burnt her in the woods of Rask. Looking down at my hands, remembering the star-cavern is Rask, and the churning howls of the beasts too deluded with the stars,

I spun around. My ribs pinched too tight around my organs, my heart trembling against them as a slow roar of realisation crept into my mind.

Einya had said she'd be done with this, one way or another, and it crashed upon me like the torrent of a storm as my footsteps faltered: *she didn't expect to survive.*

✱ ✱ ✱

Midnight, and I crept back into the forest line, having walked to the sea and back to try to convince myself not to do it. I couldn't keep myself away any longer. If she were to die, I would be with her no matter the danger of being that close to the stars.

My feet were bare as I snuck back in so as to tread softer on the moss and leaves. The moon hung high but veiled by the dense and shadow-hued canopy. It was darker, I was sure, than usual nights here. Something was stirring. The stars' eyes were moving. It almost felt as if the claws that one reached into me were there again, luring me toward the star-rock.

What are you doing? You hate the stars.

"Yes, that's true. It's just that I love her more," I said, and pressed further on with holly spiking my ankles and moss squelching between my feet.

In the darkest heart of the trees, where a gentle breeze stirred the withered firs, I found her in our hut. The little lantern swayed in the wind at the door; the sign we always left for each other to bid each other to return when one of us was wandering. Peering through the window, I saw her tangled in a blanket on the floor—the bed was empty and next to her lay the tome she'd been carving runes from. Her tousled braids lay atop it. She'd fallen asleep face forward onto the book.

I swallowed, nerves wriggling painfully up my throat. *Don't think about it.* Shoving the thought away, I looked around. How was I going to get the book? Grab it and run? *No.* Looking around, I traced my footsteps back a short way and found what I was searching for. Nestled among the thistles, sprigs of valerian poked their heads up, grey-purple and coated in the same shadows that leered over the woodland.

Was I really going to do this?

Before I could flee from my purpose, I knelt down and roughly snagged a handful of the herb and strode back to the hut. In Gemynd or Rask, these plants would be soothing only—but here in the star-spurred growth everything was stronger.

In our little hut, I poured a little water from the clay pitcher into the cast-iron kettle and hung it over the fire. Kicking off my shoes, I tugged off my stockings and threw them to the floor. The cold bare wood tingled against my toes as I waited for the whistle while I broke the valerian into a cup and mixed some honey in to mask the taste.

"I hope you don't regret this," I muttered.

Behind me, a creak of floorboards and a shuffle of paper sounded.

"Tols …?" Einya croaked, voice groggy.

Turning, placing the cup on our small rickety table, I crouched down. Wrapping her in my arms.

"I'm sorry."

"I thought you'd left me …" she whispered, and the softness of it stung my heart like a bee sting.

"I could never … I'm sorry for what I said."

Einya's trembling fingers pulled me close, and a stench of sweat clung to us both.

"It must soon be time … I don't want it to be."

"Why?" I said, easing her closer as a few patters of tears trembled onto my collarbone.

"I don't know what will happen after."

"That is for then. Can I help? If you're done with the runes, it's just reading, right? I can do that."

"Yes, but I wouldn't ask that of you. And you have to be connected to the stars …"

"And you are."

"For now," she said, pulling away and casting her eyes to the floor. The kettle began to whistle, hissing behind me: sharp and fierce to my ears.

"I'm making you tea."

"So, I see. Thank you. I didn't sleep well."

"I couldn't tell," I said, smirking, and for one moment it was like before. Joy creeping back in as a sunrise easing over a hill's crest.

We moved around in silence for a bit, Einya grabbing a few morsels of food from the cold pit dug to the side of the hut and me mixing the tea while adding more honey to mask the very distinct herbal scent.

"Please be strong," I whispered.

"What's that?"

"Nothing."

We sat, nursing the teas. Mine was honey only, and sweet enough to coat my tongue in blossom scent with each sip. I'd tipped a bit of cold water into Einya's before passing it to her, our fingers brushing as she took the steaming mug from me. In the cold of our hut, away from the fire, steam spooled from the tops of the cups.

"Tollska, I want you to know …"

"What?"

"That if this goes wrong, then …"

"Just don't say it. It can't go wrong, so much is relying on it."

We sat in silence, birds beginning to holler in the forest. Their calls, different to how I remember them sounding, seem hollow somehow. Quiet, and fading with each successive twitter.

The cup shattered when Einya rolled sideways, collapsing to the floor. It had been fast. *Too fast.* One hand in front of her mouth told me her breath was normal. Peaceful, even. *Would she wake up? No!* I couldn't think of that. I didn't know how long it would last, and I had to do it before light saturated the glade or the other astrologers found me. Heaving up the heavy tome, I shoved my finger in the page Einya had left open and closed the book on it painfully. Wincing, I didn't pause but shoved my shoulder against the door and—foolishly still barefoot—strode through the woodland to the glade where, one way or another, our fates would be decided. If one of us died, I would never let it be her. Never.

X
The Third

~ BRI ~

"It is time." Warneraii's voice shattered the silence, echoing from the shadows.

The sound jolted me awake. Gratitude twisted through my tired heart. Prethi had picked up the blade I had dropped when I fell asleep and watched Pearth intently. Flinty looks passed between them as they sat facing each other.

"What happened?" I croaked.

"Your cousin wanted me to betray you."

"What?"

"After this is done, she thought you'd try to take power for yourself."

Pushing myself up, my wrists clacked and groaned. I kept moving, despite the sharp pulse tensing my right arm as I stood.

"Pearth," I said, trying to open my arms and show no defensiveness, "If I ever wanted power, I do not want it now. I have no skill for it."

"Then you will leave it to me to rebuild?"

"I don't see many other choices."

"Enough, children!" Warneraii snapped, stepping from the shadows. "It is time."

The star, where before a softness dwelt a pressure had begun to build.

"Alright, let's not be rough with each other here," I said.

"We are too close for politeness. Look, the star begins to glow. Your sister has begun the ritual, so you must do the same. The beasts will reach us if you do not."

"Then help us do it," Pearth spat.

"I shall."

I didn't expect it, but Warneraii's stone-like fingers grasped my arm and tugged me to the star.

"Wait, I am willing. I already told you I was."

"Are you? I see love for your sister, and love for yourself. Will you do it?"

"What do you mean?" Prethi said, a trill note trembling through his voice. "What does he mean?"

"My blood is needed. Blood is always needed with the stars."

"No!"

"It is the only way. I will do it."

Prethi lurched forward, yet his strong arms could not prise Warneraii from me. Pearth just watched, a creeping smile on her face.

"Then do it," Warneraii growled, releasing my arm and thrusting a blade into my hand.

Don't pause. To pause is to decide you won't do it.

I thrust the blade across my arm, deeper than I meant until a valley of flesh form and blood flowed between like a surging rapid. Warneraii's hand guided me.

"A circle, walk."

Shuffling as best I could, teeth gritted, and my left hand gripped tightly around the dagger, I glanced at Prethi. Shaking my head, I tried to hold down a whimper, but failed. My friend wrapped his arm around me, helping me move on as my blood pattered onto the stones.

"Not enough blood. It's not working."

I sagged to the floor, my knees soaking through in the pooling crimson. I wrapped my trembling arms around Quandary.

"I'm trying, I am," I whispered. "Will any blood do?"

"Any with a connection to the stars," Warneraii said.

"So not Pearth's."

"I'd like to see you try, Bri," my cousin snarled. "I'd get that fox before you got me."

"Let's not do this …" I said, sighing. "I was only joking."

"Some joke."

"I never knew when to stop joking."

Pearth snorted.

"I am going to see to the people above. They will have heard the beasts."

With that, she turned, shrinking into the shadows to wherever the stairs up were. Returning to the star, I sliced into my arm again—trailing another spider web of blood in a circle as I walked, light flickering in my vision.

"I have to keep this going, don't I?"

Warneraii kept pace with me.

"Yes."

"Fine," I rasped, feeling everything but fine. "Prethi?"

My friend, with pinched face and clenched fists, stepped closer. "What can I do?"

"Take Quandary, keep him safe. Please."

We walked in a bizarre trio, Warneraii and Prethi untying the papoose and lowering Quandary away as I walked—scattering my circle of blood into the darkness at my feet. The star thrummed a little more with every drop, and so too did Warneraii, a strange hum coming from inside the drowned-star's flesh.

For hours I repeated this, one step in front of the other, Prethi occasionally holding me up. Pearth didn't return, presumably somewhere above with the last handful of our people.

"This can't be it," Warneraii said. It snapped me out of the foggy stupor that had faded my vision and focus. "Where is the queen?"

"I thought she would be here by now ..." I said, suppressing a shudder. *Would I be able to do it?* "She must be close."

A swirl of starlight rippled around me, and I only realised I'd fallen when I saw Prethi's face above mine from where he'd rushed over, away from Quandary. My head had struck the star-rock as I fell, and above in the sparse candlelight I could see my blood glistening upon it. The star groaned and pulse with it, a green-gold glow fizzling between the cracks in the rock.

Outside, shouts and the sound of bone scraping across metal armour and swords. The dusky scent burst through my senses.

"She's here," I rasped, and then my head lulled to one side into a brief oblivion.

✸ ✸ ✸

When I awoke, chaos churned around me like a whirlpool.

"Get up, Bri," Prethi babbled, holding Quandary close to my head so that the fox lapped away a little of the blood pooling from the cut in my hairline.

"What's happening? How long have I—"

"Not long, but long enough for everything to change."

I pushed myself up, looking into Quandary's eyes and leaning close until my forehead brushed against his fur.

"I'm still going to save you."

"We need to save us first," Pearth snapped beside me.

"You're back," I said, finally managing to get to my feet.

"The Parlentans are at the entrance, fighting the last of the beasts by the sound of it. Warneraii is helping them or keeping us safe. I'm not sure which."

"What?" I snarled. *Had the star double crossed us?"*

"Warneraii knows the queen has star-blood and will claim it back by the sounds of it."

I turned to her, daring to grip her elbow with my hand.

"Cousin ..."

"What do you want?"

"I need you to pretend I've captured you."

"What?"

"It was the condition for letting me up here. I told the queen."

"Me, I'm the condition?"

"Trust me."

"Why in star's name should I?"

"We're out of time," Warneraii called, star light bursting from the area. "The last of the beasts have fallen. She's coming."

"Help me up and then kneel, please. I promise on this we're aligned. We want our people safe. We have no choice, but to hope this works and hope Warneraii is on our side."

Pearth tipped her head to one side, tugging me up roughly.

"Only because there is no other way. Don't be haughty over this, *cousin,*" she said, sneering.

"Thank you," I whispered, as she knelt to the ground. I placed the tip of my dagger at her neck, standing over her.

"Don't push it, Briarth."

"I'm making it believable. Prethi, take Quandary to the other side of the star. Make sure he is close when the ritual completes. If it sounds like it is going badly, bring him to me. He's my last hope, my last shard of goodness."

"Bri ..."

"Do it," I snapped, teeth sharp and bared.

"This isn't like you," Prethi said, fox clutched to his chest. His eyes wide.

"We've no time for politeness, I'm sorry. Just go ..."

Prethi began to turn, head dropping so his chin grazed his chest. A small fire burnt in my chest, hollowing out my heart. *Leave it.* As if to further carve out my fragmenting heart, my friend glanced back.

"When this is done, I pray to whatever listens you remember who you are and the kindness that I … love."

I swallowed and turned away, trying not to worry about them.

"What will you do now?" Pearth asked as Prethi's hunched form lurched away into the shadows.

"What I should have done ages ago."

In the mouth of the fissure into the cave, I saw the queen. Her glistening radiance shining brightly, even in these shadows. I swallowed, pressed one hand to Pearth's shoulder until she knelt. Her sharp eyes looked up at me.

"If this doesn't work, I'll kill her. And then you."

"You may not get that chance. Besides, it'll work."

My queen—the queen—approached. Behind her, a handful of her Parlentans staggered in, all dripping in blood and ichor. Some theirs judging by the limps, some the star beasts' judging by its blackened thickness.

"Pet."

Warneraii walked behind the queen. The star was unarmed but seemed to loom taller than her, dark pits for eyes glaring into her soul as if in a moment's notice they would rip out what they wanted from her.

"My queen, I did what you bid. I have Pearth, I have the star."

"How? I do not believe you have done this. You have no-one to help you."

I swallowed. *How had I not thought of this?*

"The one behind you helped me," I said quickly, one hand running over my throat as I watched her response carefully.

"I did."

She turned.

"Who is this person? Paska only told me of you and one other."

"I had to have some help. I … found them along the way. They are Gemyndian. One of the Astrologers who, like me, sees a truer path with your rule, Glittering Queen."

The queen's lips stretched into a wider smile, but I couldn't quite see how far it spread in the shadows. I gripped one hand around Pearth's shoulder to stop my fingers trembling. Her musky floral scent dug into my nose once again.

Come closer, please, brush my cheek … touch my lips…

"You've done well."

"My Astamitra, might I have it?"

"In good time, when I have taken the star."

"Give it to me, please …" I rasped.

A tear rumbled out over the edge of my eye, strangely loud, as if the last liquid in me seeped out of me with it. Licking my lips, my throat was dry—desperately needing the liquid surging down my gullet. *I wasn't going to be able to do this.*

"You promised," Warneraii said.

"Promised what, pet?" the queen whispered, soft hand reaching up and brushing the tear away.

"Do it, Bri," Pearth ground out. "Before the guards notice."

"Oh, little lord," she said, stepping forward so quickly I didn't have time to steel myself against her soft hand gripping my chin suddenly tightly and forcing my lips to part. "You wouldn't, would you?"

"I …"

"Enough. I am tired of this. Guards, take him away."

"No, please … I did this for you."

"Traitor," Pearth spat, trying to stand, but the guards strode out of the shadows with their swords raised. "I should have known."

"I've misjudged this … and myself. I'm sorry."

I imagined Prethi's disappointed face, glowering at me from the shadows. It was Warneraii's face that glared—burning through the glittering queen and into me.

"Come with me, my queen. Astrologer … er, Warneraii, come with me also. Let's see this done."

Releasing my grip on Pearth, my hand began to quiver again. As we moved toward the star, my feet weighed heavy, dragging along the stone. The queen watched only the lightly glowing star in the centre of the cavern as we approached. *Could I do this?* The guards remained clustered around Pearth, who I thought might try something. We had to be quick.

Warneraii glared at me when we arrived by the star, the queen running one hand over it. Her sharp, talon-like nails scratched along the surface and a jitter rippled down my spine at the scraping echo.

"Sadly, the Mineral Master died," she mumbled, "so we will have to make do. Drain it for me."

"Of course," I whispered. "But first, my Astamitra. I … I need strength. Please."

"Astrologer, you drain it."

"It … is a two-person endeavour," Warneraii said next to me.

"Fine, pet, here—have your fill and get me my star-blood," she said, tucking her hand in her dress and then dangling a pouch in front of me. I grabbed it, and before I could pause, dragged my dagger from its scabbard and thrust it into her ribcage. A sharp suck of breath was all she uttered as she sagged against the blade, tugging me down with her.

As we lay on the floor, Warneraii looking down on us with interest, the queen's slate eyes flickered back open.

"I thought you wanted me ... worshipped me," she stammered, coughing blood over my face where I stood inches from her.

"Yes, I do. But I worship Luskena more."

With that, I twisted the blade again, watching as any last sap of recognition flickered out of her eyes. Burying my head in her hair, I dragged in a deep breath of her scent before tugging my hand away from the hilt and licking my fingers. *Her blood tasted of stars ... and I would miss her scent, even so.*

Behind me, the scrape of armour grating against itself echoed as her guards yelled and began to run as best they could toward me. It's too late. A stab at my heart, and the metallic taste of the stars twisted on my tongue into the touch of ashen regret.

"Warneraii ..." I rasped. "You'll have to drag her in the circle ... I can't. I ..."

"Thank you," the drowned star said, his greyed hand gripping my wrist as he smiled before tugging the queen's body from me.

"You're welcome. I can't shake the feeling that I'll regret this for all time."

"Perhaps, but that time might be shorter than you think."

"What?"

"You have star-blood in you. What did you think would happen when we completed the ritual to return the stars to their home?"

"I ..."

Warneraii was gone, carrying the body of the Queen as like a blood-sodden rag doll around the perimeter of the star as I lay upon the stones.

"Einya, this is where I found you ... this is where it began," I whispered to myself, wishing she could somehow hear me.

Another thought crept over me. *Quandary.*

Pushing myself upright, the tiny bag of Astamitra still clutched in my palm, I crawled with my limbs creaking and cracking toward the other side of the star until I found enough strength to stand and stagger the final way. Somewhere, I could hear Pearth fighting the injured guards, a clattering of steel striking dully against metal breastplates pounded like drums in the cave.

When I finally reached Prethi and Quandary, I sank back to my knees.

"What is happening, Bri?"

"It's done, or almost done," I croaked.

Looking over my shoulder, the burst of starlight had begun to thrum in the star-rocks. Glancing down, Quandary also faintly glimmered with light.

"The ritual is completing. Look how much the star glows."

"Quandary's light is so faint … will he survive?"

"I don't know, but I have something to help him. Help me pour this in his mouth."

Between us, we gently eased Quandary's little mouth open and Prethi tipped the powder in as I rubbed his chin to make him swallow.

"Thank you, little fox," I whispered, leaning forward and pressing my forehead into my saviour's russet fur. "Thank you for everything."

"Bri …" Prethi rasped.

"What?"

"Bri … you're glowing."

I sat up straight abruptly, looking down at my torso. In my chest, a pulsing glow hammered with the very beat of my heart. As the light grew, all I could see was Prethi's hands reaching up to grab my face, but even that was fading as the cavern swam with light and a strange silence that clawed down my ears. It was ending. It was all ending at last.

XI
The Fading

My tongue, leaden upon my lips, lolling out around a fuzz of foam crusting at the corner of my mouth. It was the first thing I noticed as I woke, alone on the cold floor of our small hut. Any ghost of this being a cosy, happy place faded into the ash and smoke of the burnt-out hearth.

"Bri ..." I croaked. "Is this the end of my trials?"

Groggy, I opened my eyes, rolled over so my back rested against the splintered planks, which once was rustic but now just felt shabby compared to the polished floors of Gemynd. *He's not here, and you're not there.*

Then it all crumbled down upon me. The clay beaker lay in pieces across the floor. Tollska had made that for me, and she used it to drug me ... *Tollska.* Squeezing my eyes shut, I picked up a shard of the beaker. Tightening my fingers around it, the sharp edge engraved a mark on my palm. *How could I let this happen?*

I looked frantically around for the book... It was gone.

"What have you done?"

Barefoot still, I scrabbled up from the floor and rushed to the door. Time reverberated slowly and quickly simultaneously in my mind as I ran through the woods to find the large hut where Breyneda lived. Dawn only just prickled the first crimson light through the canopy when I hammered my fist on the door.

A slow shuffle sounded inside, followed by rapid steps to the door.

"Einya? What is it?" she said, rubbing one hand over her blotchy, sleep-deprived eyes.

"The book, and Tols, are gone. She's taken it. She didn't trust me."

"Come in," she whispered, gripping my shoulder and guiding me gently in. "She wouldn't do that to you, Einya. You know that, really."

"Then where is it?"

"Maybe … maybe she is trying to help."

"No …" I spluttered, digging my nails into my leg as realisation crushed down of a different possibility. "I have to go to the star."

"I'm sure she means well."

"Are you?"

"Where are you going?"

"To do the ritual as best I remember, I have to try save Bri. There's no time."

"Einya …"

Pulling away from Breyneda, I tore out the open door. From the rustle through the leaves, I could tell she was following, but nothing slowed me down.

When I reached the glade, a tide of bile welled up in my throat and I bent over, heaving acrid yellow into the nearest foliage. My stiff neck ground as I looked back up, bent over with my hands gripped on my knees. I saw it. Saw *her*, my sweet Tollksa.

"Go to her," Breyneda whispered beside me, scooping one arm beneath mine and helping me up.

A tide of heat throbbed in my head, wavering the forest around me, but I saw the star-rock clear enough. Tollska, beside the looming menhir, rocked over the book—a torrent of barely breathed words erupting from her lips as frantic hands ran along the lines of the tome. Down her arms, large cuts into her clothing welled with crimson.

Where the vines had been cleared from the star, blood daubed the stone in a circular pattern and about the earth where I had meticulously carved runes, a phosphorescent glow thrummed through their letters. *No,… She'd done it. She'd done the ritual.*

A jagged breath surged up my throat, reaching her side. Tollska's body flinched, fog-white eyes glaring up at me as she pulled away.

"What have you done? I'm sorry," I rasped, clutching her tightly so my hands paled. "I'm sorry it came to this."

"At last, I see to know and know to see."

"What, sweet? Tols? I … I don't understand."

Fumbling, her sweat-slick hands felt their way up my face where I knelt beside her.

"I see it all, and I know. I couldn't do it anymore. I can't do it anymore."

"Do what?" I whispered. "Let me hold you, please."

A small nod, her hands dropping away to her sides. Not waiting a moment, I wrapped one arm around her and pressed my free hand to the worst of the cuts, my palm stemming the tide of blood ever so slightly.

"I couldn't keep losing you to the stars," Tollska mumbled into my shoulder.

"I'm sorry, this wasn't how it was meant to be …"

"I did it for you, for Bri and for my ma."

"Tollska, I …"

My words plunged into silence as Breyneda called my name.

"Get away!"

A crack, thunder-like, ripped through the glade. The glow of the runes, pulsing and glistening as if bejewelled by morning dew.

"Einya, what's happening?" Tols said, her fingers clutching at me.

"We have to get up, have to move."

"Why?"

"This is the final breath of the star, I think. Just help me, try and stand. I'll guide you."

Breyneda was suddenly at my side, helping Tollska from the other side until both of us had an arm each and hurriedly strode through ferns and vines to flee the glade. Turning, I saw it at last. The star-rock lifted from the earth, moss and soil tumbling from its base as it began to ascend. The soil where Tols and I had just sat fractured into a crater, tearing apart as the star tore its way from its earthen prison and up toward the gap in the canopy where once it had fallen so many years ago.

Next to me, Tollska gazed upwards—her colourless eyes moving side to side as if seeing something I could not.

"At last," she croaked, glancing at me, a speck of colour returning to her eyes. "It is done. Stay with me."

"Always, Tollska. You were always more than any star to me, and I will tell you so for our eternity."

A spark of light lifted a heavy weight from my chest as Tols nestled against me, a smile tugging the corners of her lips upwards. The first true smile in months,: maybe years. As she gripped my knee tightly and I wrapped my arms around her, the birds began to chirp in the trees. This wasn't the ending, but the beginning. The start of how things should be.

XII
The Rising

~ BRI ~

"Thank you," Warneraii's hollow voice echoed as the light pierced the cavern brightly around us.

"You promised me Luskena," I shouted. "Where is she?"

"In good time," Warneraii said, their voice drifting away.

The star's feet no longer touched the floor, arms outstretched to the sky as the ground began to quiver. Resonant trembles rattled the star-cave. Prethi, on one side of me, yelped as a deep crack split the stone floor between us.

"Over here," I said, pulling Prethi toward me.

One arm over each other's shoulders, we staggered for the gap at the end of the tunnel.

"Wait," a voice cried behind us. Pearth, her hand gripping my blood-soaked forearm.

"What?" I spat. "We need to get out."

"I can't hear you," she shouted. "The tower, the tower will come down. The last of our people are in there. Please."

Her eyes wide, and a rush of something gentler clung to my heart. "Prethi …"

"Bri, we don't have time."

"This is the last of our people. What is it all for?"

"It's too loud, but fine. Fine. I don't need to hear to understand."

The three of us clattered sideways and managed to stumble forward, steadying each other as the star-rocks began to rise. We reached the base of the stairs into the Astrologers' tower, the floor of the cave began to rip into a fissure—parting as if a seam split horizontally in the earth. The candles in the sconces tumbled to the floor, plunging us into darkness.

"You first, Bri," Prethi yelled, pushing me forward.

"No …"

"I did so much to save you. Go, don't waste it."

My feet slipped on the stairs when I tried clambering up, gravity failing as suddenly everything lurched sideways, but I eventually managed to heave myself over the crest of the spiral staircase. The marble floor, carpeted in dust, bashed the wind out of my lungs as I threw myself down and turned to shove a hand into the darkness. A rush of relief tore through me when a hand gripped back, and I heaved to pull Prethi up. Between us, with both managed to lift Pearth out of the shadows.

"It's happening too fast," she said, as we heaved her up. "The stairs are cracking."

"Then let's do this," I rasped, coughing in the growing vortex of dust surrounding us.

Screams echoed in the halls, the last score of Gemyndians running for the door to the Astrologers' grand entrance as fissures formed in the marble slabs.

"Get the vulnerable."

"Where are they?"

"In the bedrooms."

"Up the top? You have to be …" I said, grabbing my cousin and glaring at her.

"We have to do it."

"Yes," I said, beginning to run toward the stairs. "Be better if they weren't far up."

"Better than leaving them on the ground floor to be picked off by beasts or Parlentans …"

Prethi grabbed my arm, fingers searing-hot against my elbow.

"Be safe. I'll get the others out. I'll get Quandary out. Come find me."

"Stay safe," I grated, dragging him close and burying my lips briefly in his hair. "Please. You've done so much … you helped me be free. Prethi, I want …"

The ground rumbled again, and a bulge began to press through as the star scraped against the ceiling of the cavern.

"Don't say it, don't say goodbye. I can't take a goodbye. Not from you," he said, hand clutching mine as he pulled away. "Thank me later."

With that Prethi ran, and a spasm clutched my heart. What if that moment, with Prethi clutching Quandary and dashing into the shadows, was the last I ever saw him?

The thought dazed me until Pearth grabbed my elbow, jolting me out of distraction.

"I'll not forget what you've done. For now we need to work together. Sort this out."

Her eyes burnt like forge-fire, fierce and unyielding. I almost flinched away but steadied myself and turned to see the scene as the world crumbled around us. Running to the base of the wide stairs, grabbing furniture to steady us as we went. The ground rumbled beneath us as the glowing star-rock burst through the floor with Warneraii drifting above it as if guiding it upward.

"Warneraii," I shouted. "Slow this down. Help us save our people."

The drowned star's glowing eyes glared down at us.

"Be fast," the voice sounded from every nook in the tower, as if somehow the creature was everywhere.

Battling our way up the crumbling stairs, we emerged into a room with a four-poster bed slid on one angle and slumped against the tower wall. Pearth burst forward, grabbing a post and ripping the duvet away with her spare hand. *Children.* Three, cowering under the covers.

"Come on," my cousin whispered, reaching out. "It'll be okay."

Making my way to their side, I gripped onto the nearest post on the bed just in time. The room lurched sideways, and a crack sounded below.

"Pearth, the stairs …"

"I know, Bri, I know. Grab the eldest, I'll take the two youngest."

I nodded, reaching out, the child who could not have been more than ten and coughed non-stop while clinging to me.

"Let's go," I said. "If you need to swap, tell me."

"I'll be fine," she snapped. "But thank you."

Reaching the stop of the stairs, a spike of horror stabbed through me, and I turned wide-eyed to Pearth. The pitted rock glowed brightly in the mouth to the stairs, and I realised what the strange sensation between my feet was.

"We're rising. The tower is rising atop the star … I thought it would just tear through it."

"Either way, we're too late."

"We can try anyway. Come with me," I said, cradling the child closer, arms straining as blood continued to seep from them. I just about managed to reach the window. "We're not too high. Climb out."

"What? You're mad," Pearth snarled, a single tear tipping down her cheek as she clutched the two wailing children close to her chest.

"Maybe. Look after the child," I said, placing her down on the bed.

I smashed my already cut arm through the stained-glass window and clambered onto the bed. Kicking out the last of the glass, I stepped onto the slate tiles that began to shift under my feet.

"The roof is breaking, quickly. Pass me the first."

Pearth nodded, wide eyed, giving me the youngest. A boy in a dusty doublet with tattered slashing.

"What now?"

"I'll be back for the others."

With the child wrapped in my arms, I sat on the slate and propelled myself down with my legs while using my feet to slow myself at the edge. About a floor up, the star was still rising but slower. Warneraii must have given us a little time.

"Help," I shouted, and below one of the Gemyndians who'd fled the tower looked up. "Take the child."

"Have him reach out," the man beneath me yelled up.

"Okay, sorry, I don't know your name. I am going to hold your arms and lower you down."

The child sobbed, but nodded, as I held his fragile wrists gently—my belly resting on the treacherous slate tiles while I lowered them over. Everything ached in me, my arms trembling. The movement of the tower lurched, almost as if it dropped a bit lower.

Warrneraii. At least the star did something to help, even if the motion did tighten my heart and almost send me tipping over the edge. It was a moment's quick work, and the first child stood on the quivering ground of Gemynd's cobbled streets as the star and tower prised itself away.

Turning back, Pearth was climbing out of the window—helping the eldest child out behind her, the younger of the two clinging to the soldier's back. I tried to get back up to the window to reach them, but my boots slipped on the roof as I tumbled over and cracked my shoulder against a loose tile.

Behind Pearth a piercing glow burst from the windows. It would have been beautiful, pulsing through the tower's stained-glass fragments, if not for Pearth's wide, terror-filled eyes. We were out of time.

"Slide them down to me," I yelled. "I'll lower them over."

One at a time, we repeated the process. With the last child, Pearth joined me at the edge. Roof tiles were skittering off around us as we both leant over the side, one arm in each of our grips.

"She can't reach the floor," someone below us shouted up.

"Drop her the last way," I said.

"What?" Pearth rasped beside me.

"My arms are bleeding; my hands are slipping. I can't hold her. She might hurt her legs, but she'll live."

The child looked up, her eyes streaming with tears.

"Please don't," she cried, clinging to my sleeve even as the tower seemed to speed up in its rise.

"I'm sorry, it's all we can do," I said, pressing my eyes closed and opening my grip.

"Briarth, no … I can't lose another."

Opening my eyes, I saw Pearth still clinging on to the child.

"Pearth," I said, reaching to take her hand. "Each moment you wait increases that chance as we rise …"

"You are star-addled. I can't trust you," she snarled.

"Hurry," someone screamed from the cobbles. A small crowd had gathered, and I thought Prethi might be among them—a flash of sandy hair below somewhere.

"Then I am sorry, but trust me."

"No, Bri, don't."

My fingers, one at a time, pulled her fingers free. Slick with blood, it made the job easier, and the child plunged from the eave into the cluster of the remaining Gemyndians.

"How could you …"

"It was the only way."

"Did she survive? I can't see," Pearth screaming, leaning over the edge still on all fours. It would have been so easy to end it all then, and push her to her death for all she'd done…

I rolled over, trying to move from the edge, but the lurch and lean of the tower set upon the rising star made it too hard.

"Warneraii …"

"Where?" Pearth spat, crawling back from the precipice.

"Behind us. The glow is burning my neck."

As if summoned, the star emerged from the smog of the burning city.

"Yes," the drowned star said. "You have saved your people."

"And yours," Pearth growled, trying to stand. "Mostly yours."

"Yes. For that, I thank you. So, this parting gift is for you."

"What?"

"With the last of the star's gift, this is what I will do."

"You promised me Luskena …"

"Patience."

The tower lurched sideways suddenly, and I instinctively threw one arm out and gripped the lead drainpipe. My other hand shot instinctively out to steady Pearth, still trying to stand as she staggered and tipped dangerously toward the edge. Suddenly we were both tumbling sideways onto the flat roof of a nearby building. I landed sprawled on my back, gagging on the sharp intake of breath as I hit the surface. Looking up, I forgot the pain when I saw one last glance of Warneraii, the tower and the star-rocks creeping up into the clouds. I took one last deep breath of the floral scent of Astamitra that lingered in the air and licked my lips. It was *done*. I was free.

For all of that, a creeping ache tore at my heart and I gripped the flesh above it as it battered my ribcage like a drum. *Quandary*. He would be gone too. I pressed my eyes shut, a sliver of a tear teasing its way out from between my eyelids. One last moment to remember his cheeky fox-smile and smooth fur, and then I would need to face Pearth and decide what we did next.

✷ ✷ ✷

Opening my eyes, the light painfully spilt back in. The drumming in my heart battering my head as well. My cousin was slumped against the wall of an adjoining building. Her head lolled backwards and matted hair tipped over her eyes. Blood trickled over her face, and I wondered again whether this would be the moment we turned on each other, but I knew all our energy had faded.

"Pearth," I rasped. "It's done."

"No, Bri. There's so much more to do now," she mumbled, running one hand over her blooded face.

I crawled over to her, cuts all over stinging and my head faint.

"Where to start ..."

"Here, in Gemynd, where we can rebuild."

My jaw dropped slightly as I managed to slump down next to her and stretch my aching legs out. Shoulders brushing, it was almost like when we came up here as children and watched the world go by. Almost.

"In Gemynd? It is ruined. There is more left of Rask," I said, turning to her, eyes wide.

"We are Gemyndians, not Raskians."

"After all this, you will still keep us divided?" I said, stiffening at her cold, clipped statement.

She turned her head to meet my gaze, icy-laced determination glimmering in her eyes.

"I fought for this. I've battled for our identity my whole life. Do you think I would leave that now? Understand that I want to save our people."

"Our people, or our identity? There are only twenty or so here. How will they sustain a society based on that? Like it or not, you will need everyone from Rask. Make us one, make us whole."

"There will be others hidden in the ruins, and I will find them. I have to save them."

"Are you sure? Can you really gamble it all, based on that hope?" I said, looking down. From here, a carpet of beasts and other bodies were strewn in every alley and road. "We will have to live with Rask, work with Rask and blend our people with Rask's. Can't I sway you from this … single-minded path?"

"No. I will not mingle us with them; we will go back to the old ways. We survived like that for years. I fought for this," she snarled, hooking one hand into a fist as if ready to strike me. "You were the traitor. Rask will serve us again; it is the only way. You took up with Parlenta, you do not get to make decisions here."

I swallowed, a sweet memory of dusky lavender pulsing down my throat at the thought of the queen. She was dead, and I had so little left except my dream of unity. I pinched my lips tight, breathing out forcefully until my lungs were barren of breath.

Lie, Bri, finally managed to lie.

"You're right. My mind was altered by star-blood. I'm not sure who I am anymore," I said. "Come on. Let's go find them, make them safe. Everything else can come later."

"Do you mean it? I could use the help, but you'll have to accept my way of doing things."

I nodded, not trusting my tongue. Maybe after all this time, I had learnt to not say the wrong thing … finally learnt to be politic.

"I need to get these wounds tended to," I croaked instead. "I can barely move."

"Let's help each other. If we are to rebuild, I suppose I will need you. Can I trust you to follow me?"

"I will follow you," I said, accepting her hand up. Staggering to my feet, my head swam. "Remember when we used to watch Gemynd go by as children? You, me and Einya. Those were brighter times."

"They were. I'm going to climb down, then I'll help you. It's a few floors. Can you manage?"

I paused, almost saying the wrong thing. The honest thing.

"No, I'll need your help. But look, over there, there's a ladder on that building. Couldn't we go and use that? It might be easier."

"Where?" she said, turning to look where I pointed.

It was the only moment I needed, the only chance I had.

I shoved both hands fiercely against her back with a fox-like snarl. It wasn't enough. My trembling arms wouldn't shift the weight, and I felt her body tense to fight me. I pushed myself forward, thrusting my full body weight against her until the world tipped up from under us and the last thing I remember was crashing into the cobbles—my cousin's malnourished body cracking beneath me.

"Why?" she rattled, with one last breath.

"Because Rask deserves to be free," I heaved out, my eyes flickering shut as our Arden blood mingled and pooled amongst the cobble stones.

This is what Warneraii had meant by patience. He knew this would happen. He'd seen how it all ended. I'm coming, Luskena. At last, I am coming.

Epilogue

~ EINYA ~

For the second time, Tollska and I built a pyre in Rask, splintered hands piling up a plateau of wood from ruined buildings. This time we built it in the battered streets near The Dead Mule, where he'd met Luskena. No words came to me as the three of us lifted my brother onto the piles of wood, but my eyes were dry. After all this, I was just … numb. Paska had sent us word, seemingly having taken on the running of things here in the dust-laced aftermath of everything. We didn't even know how they died, all we'd found were the broken remains of my two living relatives.

Prethi sobbed next to me, and though he hadn't told me what had happened, I held him close. Paska slumped down beside us, laying a single hand on our friend's shoulder. Raskians and Gemyndians alike passed the pyre, clutches of dried flowers, heels of bread or anything they still had of some worth placed onto the wood. Finally, Prethi picked a small bundle up from the cobbles.

"It's time," Paska said, ushering him forward as she stepped up herself and placed a silver ring carved with a simple leaf upon the wood.

"Help me, Einya, please," Prethi mumbled. "He'd have wanted you to meet Quandary."

"Of course," I croaked, brusquely stepping forward, resting my head in the soft russet fur of the motionless fox whose dark eyes were open and filled with the emptiness of death. "Thank you for all you did. And to you, Prethi, thank you for all you did."

"I failed."

"No, you helped him get where he needed to go."

Between us, we placed Quandary's limp body in the cradle of my brother's arm and laid the last few wildflowers around him. Then the tears came, lancing out my stinging eyes like acid rain burning my cheeks.

"He's going to her," Tollska whispered, her eyes bright with colour again as she held me head up and kissed the tears away tenderly. "He'll be free, at last."

"He'd want that, he said once he'd burn briefly and brightly. He was right."

As night fell around us, those gathered lit torches and kindled fires in the pyre.

"For the saviour of Rask and Gemynd," some said as they lit the torches.

"No," I said, as I lowered my flame to the wood and saw the last glance of my brother as fire simmered around him. "For freedom, and the new home we will build out of these ashes. Let the old names die, we will pick something new. Something unified. That is how to remember him."

I took my torch, the last to set it to the pyre as the flames spat their sparks up into the star-strewn sky.

"Rest well, brother," I whispered.

"Let the old names die," the chant of this new country sounded, echoing into the night.

I placed the rest of my torch into the flames and returned to Prethi and Tols. While others celebrated the freedom he'd bought them as the flames painted the sky crimson, we just huddled.

"Come away, let Paska take it from here," Tols whispered, hooking me away. "Let's go to the river. My ma would be proud of you. Is proud of you. I can feel it."

I nodded, but something held me back from moving.

"Prethi, will you join us?"

"I will join you when I am ready. I have some rebuilding to do."

"Bri wouldn't want you to be alone."

"I won't be," Prethi said, shaking his head and, turning, limped into the night.

"Should we go after him …"

"Let him be," Paska whispered. "He loved Bri, but Luskena was always in the way. He needs some time to think it all through."

I froze, glancing down at her.

"You mean—"

"Yes."

"How do you know? Did Bri know?"

"It was obvious, if you looked. Luskena told me once. Bri knew, they almost … well, none of it matters now. Come away with me."

I swallowed, slowly turning away and wishing I could do more. One day I'd go back for Prethi. One last glance back at the shattered citadel, framed against a blood moon, and I was ready. I smiled as the smoke curled into the night. I turned to Tollska, who I loved that little bit more as she waited patiently for me.

"I owe you an adventure," I whispered, wrapping one arm around her waist and pulling her close.

"Every moment with you is that," Tollska smirked. "For better or worse!"

Eventually, the crisp leaves of the Raskian woods crunched under our feet as we slipped off into the treeline, unseen, free at last.

~ BRI~

My eyes drifted open, the spring sun of the fields beyond Rask stretching beyond me. The small hut I remembered in the distance, thatched with smoke pluming out of a stone chimney. Something wet nudged my hand. Glancing down, a flash of russet fur danced around my ankles. Quandary raised up on his hind legs, and nuzzled my palm with his nose.

"Thank you, little fox. For everything."

His canine grin stretched wide as he dropped back down to all fours.

"Let's go then," I said, grinning back. "One last journey."

The fox and I wove between the wheat, my palms brushing the stems until we reached the hut. I saw her, wildflowers twined in her hair in a medley of crimsons and marigold. She turned, brightness radiating around her as she smiled. I reached out to finally feel her in my arms, my eyes drifting shut as I rested my head against her cheek and brushed my lips along her chin.

"Good. You're finally here, my troublemaker."

"Home, after all this time."

We would walk and dance in peace, at last.

Acknowledgements

For the people who believed in me and the characters from *Testament of the Stars* who helped it all begin: thank you for helping the song grow.

About the Author

Alexandra Beaumont is a fantasy novelist with a passion for folklore, playing musical instruments and exploring the wilds of the UK. Her most known work, *Dissonance of Bird Song*, is praised for being a "visceral and lyrical" page turner with "praiseworthy worldbuilding" and is an Indie Ink Award Finalist for Best Setting. Specialising in gothic and folkloric literature, Alexandra's lyrical books weave together myth, magic and intrigue

MORE FROM BRIGIDS GATE PRESS

DISSONANCE OF BIRD SONG

Alexandra Beaumont

In the storm-riven wilds of ancient Cornwall the sea's whisper will charm us all.

Dissonance of Bird Song is the folkloric-fantasy tale of Eseld, a song-weaver fleeing her home to cure the sacred birds of her people and save her sister. Locked between the lies of land-dwellers and the snare of an ancient sea queen, Eseld must fight to find her own path. Amidst a storm of betrayal and heartbreak, what will Eseld sacrifice to save the ones she loves?

Readers who enjoyed Lucy Hounsom's *Sistersong*, Naomi Novik's *Uprooted*, and Natasha Bowen's *Skin of the Sea* will love *Dissonance of Bird Song*.

THE DREAMWALKER

Alethea Lyons

Harper and the gang are back.

When an opera singer is possessed by a **Dreamwalker,** the usual mayhem ensues. A ritual is set in motion that will destroy York and everyone living there, human and **supernatural** alike. Harper and team race to stop the **curse** from taking effect, but soon, they are plagued by their own troubles.

Harper's fate and family hang in the balance after her hasty oath to the River Foss. Fionn vanishes on his master's orders. Grace's brother is imprisoned.

Plus, Harper's vision shows she might be about to be kissed.

SIN:THETICA

Keith Anthony Baird

The Sino-Nippon war is over. It is 2113 and Japan is crushed under the might of Chinese-Allied Forces. A former Coalition Corps soldier, US Marine Balaam Hendrix is now a feared bounty hunter known as 'The Reverend'. In the sprawl of NeuTokyo, on this lawless frontier, he must track down the rogue employee of a notorious crime lord. But, there's a twist. His target has found protection inside a virtual reality construct and Hendrix must go cyber-side to corner his quarry. The glowing neon signs for SIN:THETICA are everywhere, and promise escape from a dystopian reality. But will it prove the means by which this hunter snares his prey, or will it be the trap he simply can't survive?

THE LEGEND OF MILDRED WELLS

Michael Clark

Formerly *The Patience of a Dead Man* trilogy

Newly remastered, re-edited, reworked, unabridged, and released as one volume

Perfect for new readers, and old fans will love the new content

After a bitter and costly divorce, construction handyman Tim Russell buys a farmhouse in the country. Aiming to renovate and re-sell, Tim's plans take a turn when he discovers the house is haunted by a fractured family whose ancient problems outweigh his own.

Tim sees a soaking-wet ghost boy and his mother, who is often seen chasing him around the house and property. Someone leaves Tim clues and burning candles, but who? Footsteps and wailing can happen anytime and anywhere. Tim, it seems, has been invited to the chaos.

Pressed into duty, Tim soon realizes he's made a mistake. He's been tricked and has started a war with a scorned dead woman, a woman whose middle name is Vengeance. Leaving is not an option.

123

Visit our website at: www.brigidsgatepress.com